Betrayed

Lillian Duncan

Cover Art by *Nicola Martinez*

Harbourlight Books, a division of Pelican Ventures, LLC
www.pelicanbookgroup.com PO Box 1738 *Aztec, NM * 87410

Harbourlight Books sail and mast logo is a trademark of Pelican Ventures, LLC

Publishing History
First Harbourlight Edition, 2014
Paperback Edition ISBN 978-1-61116-286-8
Electronic Edition ISBN 978-1-61116-285-1
Published in the United States of America

Dedication

This and all I do is for God's Glory

This book is lovingly dedicated to all those who support, encourage, and keep me writing. And no one does that more than my husband, Ronny. What a gift you are from God!

I might create the story and write the words, but without all the supporting roles my dream would be just that—a dream. Instead, I'm living my dream. How awesome is that!

Thanks first to my readers, including my friends and family. Another group of people are Christian writers who live their Christian faith not only in their writing, but by helping and supporting other writers obtain their dreams through more ways that you can imagine.

A special thanks to my publisher, Nicola Martinez at Pelican Book Group and to my editor. Jamie West, your knowledge and advice are invaluable to me.

God Bless and Good Reading.

Praise

THE CHRISTMAS STALKING (2012)

Contemporary inspirational writer, Mary Manners, winner of the 2012 IRCA for LIGHT THE FIRE: (www.marymannersromance.com): 5 BEAUTIFUL STARS... Lillian Duncan has a gift for writing romantic suspense and The Christmas Stalking is no exception. With an original storyline and characters that are rich and full of personality, she has managed to weave a plot full of twists and turns that kept me on the edge of my seat until the very last page. Now, I am only hoping for more from her!

DECEPTION (2011) A Sisters By Choice novel:

Coffee Time Romance: This suspenseful, inspirational, well-written romantic fiction is an excellent example of its genre. The key players: police, FBI agent, Patti, Jamie and Carter are people of faith, but it is integrated in such a way that it reads realistically. The pace is professional, and the characters are well drawn--a fun read.

PURSUED (2011)

Chad Young, author of *Authenticity: Real Faith in a Phony, Superficial World*: This is one of the best Christian fiction books I've read - definitely the best suspense/drama book I've read in the Christian genre. Lillian Duncan is a good writer, and her strong character is evident throughout the book.

Prologue

No way off. No way to escape. No way to get to her daughter. Why had she ever thought a yacht was a good idea for a benefit? Maria Hammond pushed her way through the throng of partygoers towards the exit. She had to get off this yacht and get to Layla before Raymond did.

"Maria."

She jerked around at her husband's voice, not believing her eyes. Raymond's arm was snaked around Patti's neck. Even from that distance, Maria recognized the panic in Patti's eyes.

Maria wanted to help, but there was nothing she could do. She had to get to her daughter. It was her only chance to keep Layla safe, to keep her away from her father. Otherwise, she would never see her child again.

Maria kept moving towards the exit ramp of the yacht.

Who was this stranger she'd slept with for so many years? She'd believed he loved her when they married, but she'd been so wrong. The events of the past month proved that—and more.

"Don't do it, Maria." Raymond's voice was low and guttural, in spite of the noise from the crowd surrounding them. She turned back as he moved the gun to Patti's head. His eyes turned black with rage. The face of evil. Why hadn't Maria seen it before? How could she have married a monster and not even known?

Her heart broken, she turned and pushed through the crowd.

No one noticed the drama happening in their midst.

Maybe, they needed to notice.

When Maria hazarded a glance back, Raymond trailed with one arm around Patti's neck. The other hand still held a gun, now pressed against Patti's temple.

Patti motioned with her hand. "Go, Maria. Just go. Don't worry about me."

Maria pointed. "Gun. He's got a gun!" Maria screamed, and then pointed at Raymond.

Heads turned.

A buzz travelled through the growing crowd.

Maria kept yelling. She couldn't do much, but she could draw attention to Raymond.

Murmuring grew louder—more partygoers panicked. People shoved and pushed as they tried to get away from the madman with the gun—her husband. Others stared and pointed.

Hatred glittered in Raymond's eyes.

It was time to go. She'd managed to turn attention to Patti and Raymond. Surely, someone would intervene. Someone would help Patti.

Gunfire exploded.

Screams erupted.

More shots.

Then a burning stab of pain. Her back. She turned.

Raymond's gaze met hers. He smiled.

Another hot burst of pain. This time in her stomach.

Have to get to Layla. Her feet wouldn't move. She swayed, and then crumpled to the deck. Her hand moved to her stomach. Wetness. Red wetness. She gasped for air. It didn't matter how much it hurt. She had to get to her daughter. She attempted to stand, but collapsed onto the smooth wooden deck. Her cheek rested against the wood, now dirty from all the feet that had walked on it that day.

Summoning strength, she moved to hands and knees, crawling. Nothing would stop her from getting to her daughter. The world suddenly turned wavy and she fought to stay conscious.

Raymond thought he had all the power, but he'd forgotten one thing.

A mother's love knew no limits.

1

He was back.

Maria's hand shook as she lifted a pink rose from the bucket and added it to the bouquet, but her gaze never strayed from the man leaning against a brown minivan across the street. It seemed as if he stared directly into the flower shop, into her eyes, into her soul.

As if searching for someone.

Her pulse raced as she memorized his features. Shaggy beard. Longish, sandy blond hair. Average height. Average build.

She took a deep breath. *Calm down. It's just your paranoia. It's not real.*

Her imagination was running wild…again.

He was probably some local man waiting for his wife or a friend to finish shopping.

Please, let him have nothing to do with us. Let him be a harmless husband waiting for his wife.

But if that was the case, why was it the third time in as many days she'd seen him?

That couldn't be a coincidence.

Could it?

The first time she'd noticed him, he was walking out of one of the many antiques stores that surrounded the square of Sunberry. The second time, he'd been sitting at the Coffee Cup's outside table sipping one of their fancy concoctions. And now, he sat across from her shop staring in her direction.

Whenever she saw him, she kept her face averted, but his gaze moved from one person to another— always searching.

Stop being so paranoid.

She picked several more flowers to add to the bouquet.

Again.

What other explanation could there be?

Her nightmare would never be over. Raymond warned—no, promised—that she'd never be free of him. That he would win. That she would never be allowed to raise Layla as an American.

She didn't want to leave Sunberry. It was their third location since entering Witness Protection. Layla needed some stability, and Maria thought this was the right place.

This was where Layla could grow up free from fear.

Maria loved the flower shop. She wanted to believe being surrounded by the beauty of the flowers every day would erase the ugliness she'd experienced.

No sane woman would ever forget the betrayal of a man she'd loved and whom she thought loved her.

Betrayal was an understatement. Maria didn't have a word big enough to describe what Raymond had done to her—and to Layla, their daughter. She forced the pain away. Better to keep it dead and buried—just like her name, her past, and her identity.

She walked back to the sales counter and focused on the man across the street.

"Everything OK, Veronica?" Conrad's voice brought her back to the present.

"Sure, why do you ask?" Her new name always

gave her an internal pause, a fraud that had to be continued for Layla's safety.

"That's not what I asked for." Conrad pointed at the flowers in her hand.

Her gaze moved to the bouquet. Instead of the dozen pink long-stemmed roses he ordered, she held a hodgepodge of different flowers.

Her cheeks heated up. "I'm so sorry. I don't know what I was thinking. It will just take a minute to fix."

"You seemed worried."

His eyes were warm and kind. Not cold like Raymond's.

"OK, those will be fine," he said with a grin. "Don't worry about it."

She looked at Conrad, one of the local police officers. The uniform he wore should've made her feel safe, but it didn't.

Nothing did.

She laughed. "That's nice of you, but I don't think so. My customers get what they want." She held up the bouquet. "Not a mess like this. It will only take—"

"This is fine. Really." He touched her arm in a comforting gesture.

A shiver ran up her spine, causing confusion. She sputtered an answer. "Well, then, they're on the house. Your wife or girlfriend must love flowers. You're one of my best customers."

"Is that a sneaky way of finding out if you had coffee the other day with a married man?" A grin tugged at his mouth.

"I just assumed the coffee was about business. Your sneaky way of finding out about the new business owner in town. Making sure I'm..." Her words faltered, not sure how to finish the statement without giving him cause for suspicion. "Making sure I have the town's best interests at heart."

"Actually, the flowers are for my mother. And our coffee date wasn't about interrogating the new business owner. It was about getting to know you. You don't have any secrets lurking behind those beautiful brown eyes, do you?"

She forced her gaze to meet his, hating the fact she couldn't be honest with anyone. How was she supposed to make friends when she had to lie to them all the time? "No secrets that you need to know about." Her cheeks flamed at her flirtatious come back. In a more serious tone, she said, "No. Of course not. I was...never mind. Anyway, you must be a good son."

"It's the least I can do for her. After all I put her through, she deserves a medal."

Maria wrapped the bouquet in pink tissue paper and then handed it to him. "Instead all she gets are these crazy flowers. Hey, that's a great idea. I'll call this my crazy quilt bouquet. And I can use all my leftover flowers to make it. What do you think?"

"And I'm the first to get one. I'm honored." He handed her a twenty.

Not taking the offered money, she shook her head. "On the house, really."

"Can't. That could be construed as a bribe, ma'am." He winked. "And here in Sunberry we don't do things like that."

The twenty passed between them. As their fingertips touched, she felt another tingle.

"The crazy quilt bouquet's a good idea. Of course, I think you should create a 'Go Bucks' bouquet." He grinned, obviously a fan of the football team.

"Scarlet and gray carnations." She wrinkled her

nose and then counted out his change.

"What's wrong with scarlet and gray?" Conrad asked in a mock serious tone. "I happen to think they are a beautiful color combination."

"You and all the other Ohio State fans."

"That's my point. I think they'd be a big seller."

"I will take the matter under consideration when football season comes around."

"Don't you like football?"

"Doesn't everyone?"

"You aren't a fan of that state to the north, are you?"

"Oh my, no." She laughed. "That would be wrong on so many levels."

"I've got season tickets for OSU. Maybe you'd like to go to a game with me—sometime."

Uh-oh. Time to nip the flirting. Having coffee with him was one thing, but going on a real date—and to an Ohio State game at that—was probably not a good idea. "Thanks for being so understanding about the flowers."

He nodded. "Not a problem. But you looked so worried a minute ago. Are you sure everything's OK?"

Her gaze moved to the street. The shaggy man was not in her line of sight any longer. Had he moved down the street?

"Yes, I'm OK." She hoped her tone was steady.

"See you soon, Veronica." Conrad turned to leave. "And don't forget about the Bucks Bouquet. It even has a nice ring to it."

"Who could forget that?"

"It'll be a big seller. Trust me."

Her gaze met his. "I don't do trusting."

"That's no way to live."

"I tried it once. It didn't work."

"Everyone needs to trust."

"Oh, I trust God and myself." She paused and gave him a grim smile. "But truth be told, most days I don't trust myself all that much, either."

"Well, God's the right choice, anyway. He won't let you down like people." He pointed at his badge with a wink. "And you can trust me. See you soon, Veronica." The bell above the door tinkled as he left.

She breathed out a sigh of relief. Next time he came in, she'd need to be more professional. She had no plans to have a relationship again—ever.

Good thing he'd been so nice. Another customer would have complained. She needed to keep her mind focused if her flower shop was to be successful. The pittance Witness Protection gave her was enough to get by—just barely.

She should take a picture of the man out in the square. Why hadn't she thought of that earlier? She walked out of the flower shop. He was gone, along with the van he'd been leaning against. Maybe she should have told Conrad about him. She'd been tempted to, but what could she say without sounding paranoid?

Don't act paranoid around others. They'll wonder what you're hiding. That had been one of the nuggets of wisdom from the Witness Protection people.

As she walked into The Bouquet, she caught a glimpse of herself in the store's window. There was always that one quick second when she was surprised at her new look.

Instead of the thick, long black hair she'd been born with, her hair was now short and blonde. She'd lost twenty pounds by running and weightlifting.

Instead of the slightly plump housewife she'd been, she was now slender and a lean, mean fighting machine.

If they tried to steal Layla from her again, she'd be able to protect her daughter.

Looking at her reflection reminded her that Maria Hammond was as dead and buried as her husband. Veronica Minor had risen from the ashes with hope of a new life, but her hope faded a little more each day.

Transitioning to life as a new person wasn't easy. Some days, she could barely function with the fear that always lurked. It was getting harder to leave their apartment to go to work, to shop, to go to church.

Plain and simple, she was a mess.

But Layla was happy. She loved her new school and already had two best friends.

Maria pretended to be happy when Layla was around. She had no idea how much longer she could fool her daughter. Maria walked back into the store.

There was work to be done, but her gaze strayed outside, searching for the man or anyone else who seemed too interested in the flower store.

Her stomach clenched.

This wasn't going to work out—again. They promised her she was safe, and a part of her believed them. But the other part was winning.

At night, she dreamed of Raymond's glittering black eyes. During the day, flashbacks would take her back to those terror-filled days when he'd stolen Layla from her.

The U.S. Marshals at the Witness Protection Program wouldn't be happy when she requested another move, but she didn't care. It was her responsibility to keep Layla safe. She'd failed her daughter once, and that would never happen again.

Time to call Morgan Reed.

It wouldn't be pleasant.

Her knees weakened as she walked to the door and turned the sign from open to closed, then locked it and set the security system. She slid her cell phone from her pocket and hit Morgan's number. It was on speed dial.

"Good morning, Veronica. How are you today?" Morgan refused to call her Maria any longer.

Her voice was cheerful, but Maria knew the woman wasn't happy to hear from her. "Not so good."

"What's the problem now?"

"A man has been watching me for the past three days."

"Did you get a picture of him? I can run it on facial recognition."

"I went outside to get it, but he disappeared."

"Probably just waiting on someone near the store."

"I've seen him the past three days."

"Veronica, I warned you to go to a bigger city than Sunberry. You're bound to see the same people over and over when you live in a small town. That doesn't mean they're out to get you. Small town living is like that. You know everybody and everybody knows you."

"We need to move."

"Not going to happen. We went through this. Unless there is a credible threat, I can't move you again. Witness Protection can't move you every two months. It doesn't work that way."

"So, what's a credible threat? After they kill me? After they kidnap Layla? When does it become a credible threat, Morgan? Tell me that."

A pause. Maria could imagine Morgan rolling her eyes. The woman didn't take anything she said seriously. They hadn't been a match from the first time they'd met. She'd always felt like Morgan thought she'd been involved with Raymond's activities.

"Of course not, Veronica. I'm concerned, just as you are." The right words, but the wrong tone.

"You always discount what I say."

"That's not true. We haven't had any proof that they found you, but we've moved you each time you requested."

"I'm requesting it now."

"It's not my call. I'm not the one who made the decision. If we have any sort of proof, even a slight indication, I'll make them change their mind. If the man comes back get as many pictures as you can. I'm sorry, that's the best I can do. My hands are tied. The offer for counseling still stands."

"Thanks." Maria took a deep breath and hung up.

She and Layla were leaving. With or without Witness Protection's help. She'd close the shop, pick up Layla from school, get their escape bags, and disappear. Heading for the back door, her feet slowed. Maybe she was paranoid.

Raymond's betrayal had stolen her trust. She no longer had any confidence in her own ability to make the right decisions.

She didn't want to make Layla leave again if it wasn't truly necessary.

Layla loved Sunberry. Her daughter would be hurt if they moved again. All Maria wanted was keep Layla safe, let her have a normal childhood. It wasn't fair to keep uprooting her.

Maria closed her eyes, summoning strength she

didn't have.

Please God, give me wisdom.

It was up to her to make a real life for Layla. Her sweet, trusting Layla. Her daughter had no idea there were people out there who wanted to kill Maria. Or to steal Layla and take her far away so Maria would never see her daughter again.

Maria slid to the floor behind the counter, sobbing.

2

Maria lost track of time as she cried and rocked back and forth. She had to get a grip on her life—if not for her then for Layla.

Maria couldn't go through life being afraid every time someone stared at her a moment too long. Or approached her to talk. Or tried to be her friend.

She believed *in* God, but now it was time to *believe* God and all the wonderful promises she'd read in His Word.

She wouldn't be intimidated by faceless, nameless bullies any longer.

She stood up, straightened her shoulders, and went to the tiny bathroom to freshen up.

Returning to the front of the store, she stiffened her spine. The scent of the flowers wafted through the air. She took a deep appreciative breath.

Beauty for ashes. One of God's promises.

Her hand touched the "Open For Business" sign as she stared out at the picturesque square. When the U.S. Marshal had shown her the photo of Sunberry's square, she knew she could be happy here.

A huge white gazebo sat in the middle of the town square. On summer nights the local talent gathered to entertain citizens. The square was surrounded by an old brick road where the patrons of the local antiques stores and other quaint shops parked the old-fashioned way.

Sunberry seemed a million miles from the bustle of big cities, but it was less than an hour from the capital of Ohio. She'd wanted a place where she and Layla could be part of the community since they'd never see their own family or friends again.

Unfortunately, she was still as alone as the day they moved to town. But it was her own fault. People reached out to her, but she'd shunned their efforts, afraid to trust.

Maria closed her eyes in a wordless prayer and felt strength seeping into her spirit. *I won't let Raymond win. He isn't going to steal my daughter's joy or innocence. No more.*

A smile played on her lips as she flipped the sign to open.

After reopening the flower shop, Maria focused on work. She paid bills, ordered supplies, and even had a few customers. Of course, she kept checking for the man, but he didn't show up again.

Several hours later, two girls came skipping down the street, one dark-haired and the other a blonde. The girls reminded her of a whirlwind of leaves on a breezy fall day. So happy and carefree. Her eyes filled with tears at the giggling girls, glad she'd decided to stay in Sunberry, for now.

Thanks for the courage, God. Keep it up. Please.

She walked outside to greet them. "Hi, Jasmine." She bent down to give Layla, now Jasmine, a hug, and then looked at the other girl. "Hello, Emily. How was school today?"

The little blonde girl grinned up at her with two front teeth missing. "It was good, Mrs. Minor." She held up a chubby hand and opened it. "I lost another tooth today."

"So you did. Would you like to come in and eat a snack with Jasmine?"

Layla put her hands on hips and gave Maria a disgusted look. "Mom, you're supposed to call me Jazzy, remember? Not Jasmine."

"I'm sorry. Would you like to share a snack with Jazzy?"

"I can't. Mommy is waiting for me. We're going to go buy some new shoes, and then have pizza. Girls night out, she said. Daddy has to work late and the boys are busy with baseball practice."

"Sounds fun."

"Can Jazzy come with us? I know Mommy wouldn't care."

Her daughter's chocolate brown eyes lit up with anticipation. "Yeah, Mom. It would be so fun. Can I?"

Maria's mind flashed back to the man staring at the flower shop. "Not tonight, sweetie. It's a school night. Some other time."

"Oh, Mom. I never get to have fun." Jasmine whined, but stopped as Maria gave her "the look." She turned back to her little friend. "Sorry, Emily. Maybe you can stay at my house on Friday night."

"Yeah, that sounds like a great idea." Maria agreed. "Ask your mom about it tonight, and then we'll make plans later in the week."

"OK." Emily waved before skipping down the street with blonde hair bouncing behind her.

Layla grabbed Maria's hand, the girl's cheeks rosy red with excitement, her disappointment at missing girls' night out already forgotten. "Guess what happened today, Mom?"

I don't know. What?" Hand in hand, they turned towards the store.

"No, you have to guess. You'll never guess in a million, billion years."

As she opened the door to the shop, a movement in her peripheral vision drew her attention. Her head jerked towards the street.

Empty. Emily must really be in a hurry to go buy those new shoes. She hurried her daughter into the flower shop. "So, tell me. What happened?"

"You have to guess."

Maria followed Layla into the store. "You got an A on your spelling test?"

Layla giggled. "Well, I did, but that wasn't the right guess."

"You had pizza for lunch?"

"No, Mom. You gave me a peanut butter sandwich for lunch. You know that."

"Oh. I forgot. I can't imagine what happened today. Just tell me."

"I'll give you a clue. Maybe then you'll figure it out."

"OK, what's the clue?"

The bell above her door tinkled.

A young woman walked in. She was thin and her brown hair looked as if it needed a shampoo. The girl smiled, but looked nervous. "Hi."

Maria smiled back. "How can I help you?"

"I...uh...I wondered if you were looking for help. I can do anything. Clean up, or deliver flowers, whatever you need me to do."

"Oh, I'm sorry. I don't need any help." She was barely making a living for her and Layla from The Bouquet.

The smile stayed on the girl's face, but her shoulders slumped. She walked towards the door with a mumbled, "Thanks, anyway."

Maria touched her shoulder before she could slip out the door. The girl looked at her, eyes glistening with unshed tears.

"Are you OK?"

She nodded, but a tear leaked out. She quickly wiped it away. "Just need a job. Don't worry about it."

"Are you sure?"

"I'm fine." The girl walked out.

Maria stared out at the girl. Her intuition said the girl was in trouble. She hurried to the door. "Hold on a minute."

The young girl turned back towards her.

"I do get busy on Saturdays. Why don't you come this Saturday and we'll see how it works out?"

The girl nodded; her eyes brightened. "Thanks. I'll be here at eight."

"Make it seven thirty. And no promises."

"Sure, no problem."

With a smile, Maria walked back in the store where Layla was waiting with her little hands on her hips. "It's my job to help you on Saturdays."

"And you still will, but she looked as if she needed assistance. And what's our rule about helping others?"

Layla's head twisted and she grinned. "We always help people if we can."

"Good girl. Now...tell me what happened to you today. I'm all out of guesses." She leaned in and put her arms around her daughter, and then tickled her. "Now, tell me. No hints. No guesses, just tell me, Jazzy girl."

Layla giggled. "No, never."

After more tickles and laughter, Layla relented. "OK. OK, I'll tell you."

Maria removed her hands. "I'll stop, but I'm warning you. I can catch you if I need to tickle the answer out of you."

Layla held up a hand. "OK. OK, I'll tell you, but I think you're going to be surprised." She paused dramatically, eyes shining. "I saw Daddy today."

3

I saw Daddy today.

Maria's mouth turned to sand as the words fell from Layla's mouth. Her mind went numb, and she wasn't sure if she would be able to take her next breath.

Layla smiled up at her, her eyes bright with the innocence of a child.

"What did you say?"

"I saw Daddy today."

The once fragrant smell of the flowers turned sickening. Her stomach churned. *Was it possible? Could Raymond still be alive?* Impossible.

Marcus Hanks assured her he was very dead, but she hadn't actually seen his dead body…maybe they lied.

But why?

The FBI would have nothing to gain by lying to her, would they? She'd been cooperative. Not that she knew much. She'd been blind to his nefarious activities.

Her heart raced. She wanted to grab up her daughter and run. Sweat oozed out of her palms. *Don't panic. Stay calm. Keep breathing.*

"Honey, we've talked about this before. Remember what happened to Daddy?"

As she waited, she looked around the flower shop. They would need to leave.

"He went to heaven. That means he's an angel now. I saw his angel today. He was watching me. Daddy must miss me, don't you think?"

Maria forced a smile in spite of the sick feeling in the pit of her stomach. She'd need to explain to Layla that people didn't turn into angels. That God created the angels as individual beings just as He created humans, the flowers, and the trees. But that could wait until later. Now she needed to listen to Layla. "Can you tell me what happened?"

"I was playing outside at recess. I looked over, and Daddy was standing on the sidewalk staring at me."

Maria's heart raced.

Surely, Layla would know her own father.

"Did he do anything? Say anything?"

"He waved at me so I started walking over to him, but he disappeared. Into thin air. That's why I know it was Daddy's angel. People don't just disappear into thin air, but angels can."

"No, people can't just disappear, sweetie. You're right about that." *Stay calm.* If she panicked, she would upset Layla.

Was this her daughter's imagination gone wild?

"Are you sure it wasn't just someone who looked like Daddy?"

"Nope." Layla was firm. "It was Daddy's angel."

They were definitely going to have a talk about that—later.

"Ready for that snack?" Her voice was calm, but her mind was flitting around like a moth to a light bulb. Not wanting to alarm her daughter, Maria managed to act composed as she walked to one of the flower coolers where she kept Layla's afternoon snack.

****

Time to go home. Her nerves were frazzled. Maria needed time to decompress.

Could Layla really have seen Raymond? If Raymond really was alive, he would have grabbed Layla and the two of them would have disappeared together. She wouldn't have even known there was a problem until hours later. No, it wasn't Raymond.

But it could have been someone who looked like Raymond. Perhaps his family wanting to steal Layla away from Maria. Certainly, they would want to raise Raymond's daughter as their own.

She shut the thought down.

No. it wasn't true. It was her imagination and paranoia running wild again.

Layla must have imagined it, but that was a worry. Was Layla on the verge of some sort of breakdown?

Maria needed an expert's opinion. It was time to talk with a child psychologist. She'd call Morgan Reed in the morning to arrange it.

It felt good to make a decision.

First, Raymond controlled her, and now Witness Protection did.

Her life still wasn't her own. It was time to take back her life—and Layla's.

For the second time that day, Maria walked to the flower shop's door, locked it, and armed the security system. She turned to leave, but a movement on the sidewalk caught her eye.

Two uniformed police officers walked towards her with grim faces.

Now what?

After disarming the security alarm once again, she

opened the door to the two waiting officers, a man and a woman.

"Hi, Veronica."

"Hi, Conrad. Are you here for a refund? Didn't your mother like the flowers?"

"She loved them. It seems like your crazy quilt bouquet is a hit."

The female officer stepped forward. She was of average height with dark blonde hair. "We need to speak to you." She glared at her partner for a moment. "And it's not about your flowers."

"Can I see some ID?"

The woman exchanged a look with Conrad. "What—the uniforms and the police cruiser aren't enough for you?"

"Sorry, I didn't mean it to sound like that. Can't be too careful these days." Maria smiled sweetly, but the woman didn't return one.

Conrad caught her eye and winked. His salt-and-pepper hair and glasses gave him a look of wisdom, while his smile gave her a sense of reassurance.

"Got a reason to be worried?" The female officer asked.

"No, of course not." Maria wouldn't tell the woman about Layla seeing her dead father.

"Good, let's go inside and talk."

"Officer Zinkleman, show the lady your ID and stop acting like a hard...hard case."

Officer Zinkleman glared at Conrad and Maria, but she pulled out her ID and handed it to Maria.

Layla peeked out from behind her mother. "Hi, I'm Jazzy. Don't be mad. My mommy worries a lot since my daddy went to heaven. My daddy's an angel now."

Conrad squatted down to Layla's height. "It sounds like your mommy is quite the smart lady. It always pays to be careful, doesn't it, Officer Zinkleman?" His tone was even, but Maria detected a slight reprimand. "This is my partner, Officer Suzanne Zinkleman. And you already know me." He held out a hand and covered hers in a warm and reassuring touch.

She looked away, relishing the pleasant physical reaction she had to this handsome man. But it was a complication she didn't need or want.

Maria checked the badge, and then handed it back. "Thanks. Like my daughter said, I'm a little bit paranoid these days, Officer Zinkleman."

"Not a problem." Her tone warmed ever so slightly. "Just call me Suzanne or Zink. Everybody does. This is a small town. We don't stand on formalities around here."

"OK, Suzanne it is."

"We're actually here for a reason." Suzanne's gaze moved to the flower shop as if indicating that was the place for the talk.

"Let's go inside." Maria took the hint, opened the door to The Bouquet and let the officers walk in ahead of her. What could the police want with her?

"When was the last time you saw Emily Most?" Conrad asked.

"Emily? You mean La...Jasmine's friend?"

Zink nodded, scrutinizing Maria.

"Why do you want to know about Emily?" Layla stepped in front of her mother. "Is she OK?"

"You know what, Jazzy?" Officer Zinkleman touched Layla's shoulder. "I would love a bouquet of flowers to take home. Can you help me pick some while your mother talks with Officer Conrad?"

"I can do that." Jasmine squared her shoulders and asked, just like she'd heard her mother do so many times, "Exactly what will the flowers be for?"

Suzanne Zinkleman chuckled as the two of them walked away. "Just something pretty for my house."

"What happened to Emily?" Maria lowered her voice as she looked at Conrad.

"Emily never made it home after school."

"But that was over an hour ago. It's a five minute walk from here. She doesn't even have to cross any streets."

"I know."

A chill ran down her spine. "The girls always ride the bus and walk this far together. And then Emily goes the rest of the way by herself."

"Are you sure they walked home together today?"

"Absolutely. Emily was here. She didn't come inside, but we talked outside for a minute." She nodded. "I asked her to come in for a snack, but she said she had to get home. She was going shopping with her mom for shoes."

"And where was she the last time you saw her?"

She walked to the window and pointed. "Right about there. She was skipping towards her house when we came into the store."

Children weren't supposed to disappear here. That's why she'd chosen a smaller town. She wanted Layla to grow up in a safe environment. A place where she could play with friends without being afraid.

Tears welled up as memories of Raymond kidnapping Layla surfaced. She pushed them aside. Time to focus on Emily. "What do you think happened?"

"We're not sure yet. It could be nothing. She might be over at a friend's house and forgot to call her mom. The parents are calling everyone, but they mentioned Emily and Jazzy usually walk home together so we decided to come talk with you before everyone gets in a panic."

"What can I do to help?"

"I know there's some volunteers from their church out looking already. I'm sure they would appreciate your help. You didn't see anything unusual today? Anything that set off a red flag?"

Her stomach flip-flopped, remembering the man across the street. But he'd been staring at her. It couldn't have anything to do with Emily. Emily hadn't been around any of the times she'd seen him. And besides it had been her paranoia, hadn't it?

Officer Zinkleman and Layla returned.

Zink held a beautiful bouquet of bright red carnations mixed with pink miniature roses and white baby's breath.

Maria admired the flowers. Her daughter had a good eye. Maybe, she had chosen the right profession for their new life.

"We need to ask Jasmine a few questions." Conrad lifted a brow, asking silent permission.

Her stomach churned, but she nodded.

Hopefully, Layla wouldn't say anything to give away their secret.

He stooped down to Layla's height. "Emily didn't come home after school and we're worried. I wondered if you might know where she is."

"She said she was going home so she could go shopping with her mom, remember?" Layla's gaze flitted to Maria's with a confused look.

She touched her daughter's shoulders. "I do remember, honey. That's why it's important to answer the policeman's questions."

"Was she mad at her mom or dad?" Conrad added.

Layla's brown hair swayed as she shook her head.

"Where would she go if she was mad at them?"

"I don't know." Layla shrugged. "Maybe to our apartment, but that would be a long walk."

"That's good. Anywhere else she might go?"

"Dina's."

He nodded. "We'll be sure to check that out. Did anybody follow the two of you here as you walked from the bus stop today?"

"No."

"Any other day?"

"No."

"Did anything unusual happen at all today?"

"I saw my daddy's angel. But he wouldn't hurt Emily. I miss my daddy."

Officer Conrad Travis looked at Maria.

She tilted her head and narrowed her eyes in warning, silently begging him not to ask Layla anything more about it.

"OK, good job, Jasmine." He stood up. "I have one more question for your mommy, and then we'll go find Emily."

"I like to be called Jazzy."

He smiled at her. "OK, Jazzy. It was nice to meet you."

Maria stepped away from Layla.

"What's that about?" He whispered, as Zink distracted Layla with a question about the flowers.

"I'm not sure. Today's the first time she's talked

about seeing her Daddy's angel. I was planning to call someone about it when I got home."

"You mean like a child psychologist, or something?"

"Something like that. She was very close to her father and misses him."

"Mmm. How long ago did he die?"

"Less than a year."

"I'm sorry for your loss." His gaze met hers.

"It's a loss for Jasmine, not for me. Our marriage was over." Her face warmed as she wondered why she'd bothered to tell him that.

"Still, it has to be hard," he murmured. "Thanks for your help. Are you going home?"

"Yes."

"If Emily happens to be there, please let us know."

"Of course."

Officer Zinkleman held up the flowers. "How much for these?"

"That's not necessary," Maria said. "Take them as a gift."

"Can't do that. It's not ethical these days."

"Fill this out and I'll send you a bill." Maria pulled a slip out from a drawer. "The register's closed down for the day."

Zink began to fill out the form. "You have a beautiful daughter," Officer Zinkleman said. "She seems very smart and sweet."

"Thanks. I think she's wonderful." Maria smiled.

"Make sure you send me that bill, Veronica."

Maria and Layla watched the officers leave.

Layla turned to her, worry in her chocolate brown eyes. "Mommy, where's Emily? Why can't they find her?"

Dread rose in Maria's heart.
She had no answer.

4

Emily wasn't at their apartment. Maria hadn't expected she would be, but to ease Layla's mind they'd checked it anyway. Poor Layla, disappointment had shone in her eyes when it was obvious Emily wasn't waiting for them.

Maria drove to Emily's house to help with the search.

Cars lined both sides of the normally quiet neighborhood, and small groups crowded the street.

"Mommy, why are there so many people here?"

"Because everyone's worried about Emily, honey."

"So am I, Mommy. Where could she be? What do you think happened to her?"

"I don't know, but we'll help look for her. Will that make you feel better?" She glanced into the rearview mirror at her daughter.

Layla nodded.

"Good."

In spite of the approaching darkness, camera crews' lights brightened the neighborhood as if it was noon. They must have driven in from Columbus.

Maria studied the news crew from her vantage point, making sure no cameras pointed their way. She didn't need to complicate their lives by appearing on national TV. Hand in hand, she and Layla walked through the Mosts' backyard.

A man stepped out of the shadows. "Can I help

you?"

Maria yelped.

Layla giggled.

"Sorry, didn't mean to scare you, ma'am. I'm trying to keep the media at bay. They're trying to sneak in any way they can."

"We came to help. My daughter is a school friend of Emily's." She pointed at Layla. "I own The Bouquet."

"Oh, the new flower store."

"That's the one."

"Nice place. My wife is always hinting about getting flowers. Guess I should stop in sometime."

"Women love getting flowers. They didn't find Emily yet?"

"No, and it's crazy here. I've never seen anything like it." He shook his head. "I'm standing guard. The TV people are swarming the area. A while ago, one was caught filming through a window. Can you believe that?"

Maria nodded. "I can." The media frenzy after Raymond's unmasking on the yacht was life-changing for her and Layla. "I know they have a job to do, but it's not one I would want."

"Amen to that." He scanned the area. "Please wait here." He disappeared inside the house.

"Why can't we go in, Mommy?" Layla was impatient.

"Because he has to make sure we're really their friends."

The policeman came back and motioned them in.

Layla held her hand and led the way.

Maria's courage almost failed her. It was important to be a good model for Layla, and it was time to stop being so afraid.

Mrs. Most's hair was disheveled and her eyes were red, but she smiled when she saw Layla. "Hi, Jazzy."

Layla hugged her. "Did you find Emily, yet?"

Tears leaked from her eyes, but Mrs. Most wiped them away. "Not yet, but everybody's out looking for her. Hopefully, we'll find her soon."

"We went to our apartment and looked for her, but she wasn't there."

"Thanks for trying, sweetie."

"I'm so sorry." Maria said. "We came to help search for her. I'm...Jasmine's mother, Veronica Minor."

Mrs. Most nodded. "Thanks for coming. We're so grateful for..." Her hand motioned towards the others. "For everyone who's helping. It's amazing. The local pizza shops are bringing food and drink in for the volunteers. Everyone is so..." She gulped back a sob. "I sure hope we find Emily soon. She doesn't like the dark."

"This is so horrible, but I'm sure they'll find her soon." She handed Mrs. Most a business card. "Here's my phone number. You call me if you need anything. Really. I'll help in any way I can. Do you need someone to babysit your other children?"

"No, they're older. In fact, they're out driving around looking for Emily right now. She's...our baby." The last words came out in a sob.

Mr. Most's arm enclosed his wife, and she laid her head on his shoulder.

"I'm going out to the volunteer table and see what I can do."

"Thanks so much," Mr. Most said.

Layla had slipped away while Maria talked with

the Mosts.

Outside, Layla stood in front of a group of cameras talking with a news reporter about Emily and asking viewers to look for her friend.

Panic hit Maria so hard she stumbled as she ran towards her.

Layla couldn't be seen on TV.

Maria rushed over and stood between her daughter and the camera.

The news woman glared at her. "Hey, we're doing a broadcast here."

She shielded Layla from the cameras. "Not anymore, you aren't. You can't film her without my permission and you cannot broadcast the segment, either. Turn the camera off."

The newscaster made a slashing motion across her neck to the cameraman. "Too late. It was live." The newscaster shrugged. "She's the one who came up to me. She's very worried about her little friend. I assumed she had permission."

"Sure you did."

"She's adorable, by the way. People will stop as they're walking past their TV, just to see what the cute little girl is doing on the news. When they hear she's out looking for her missing friend, they'll want to look for her, too. It could make all the difference."

Maria wondered if she was sincere. She almost believed the newscaster cared.

But Layla being on TV could be very dangerous.

"Make sure the piece doesn't run again or I'll sue." She stared at the woman with an unflinching gaze.

The news reporter blinked, her face red. "Sorry for the misunderstanding."

"Come on, honey. Let's go look for Emily."

5

Conrad Travis stood in the shadow of the tree watching the ever-growing media circus. There were too many people and too little organization to be effective.

This was not the way to find Emily Most.

He'd been impressed when Veronica Minor and her daughter showed up a while ago. Remembering the haunted look in her eyes that morning as he bought flowers, his gut said there was a story behind the woman's gaze.

He'd enjoyed the time they'd shared over coffee a week earlier. He hadn't dated since the death of his wife two years ago, but Veronica's smile made him think it might be time to get back in the swing of life.

Zink walked up and handed him a cup of coffee and a slice of pizza on a napkin. "I thought you might be hungry."

"I'm not." He took the pizza from her. "But I'll eat it, and then I'm leaving. Nothing's getting accomplished here."

"Sure it is. Every politician within a fifty mile radius is getting their picture on the news."

"And how exactly is that helping Emily?" He bit off a piece of pizza and chewed.

"Didn't say it was. What's your plan?"

"I'm going to the station to get a list of every sexual predator in this county and all the surrounding counties. Then, I'm going to go visit every one of them."

"That could take all night."

"Yep. It could."

"Then, let's get started."

6

Guilt stabbed Maria.

Emily might not be missing right now if she'd walked her to the corner. It had been a mistake to dismiss her own feelings as paranoia.

The stranger across the street.

Layla seeing her dead father.

Emily missing.

Maria had decided the lurking man was her imagination. Layla seeing her father had been Layla's imagination, but Emily going missing was nobody's imagination. It was reality.

Could they somehow be connected? It didn't seem plausible, but Raymond being a terrorist hadn't been plausible, either. So she wasn't exactly the best judge of character.

She and Layla had searched the section assigned to them. In each alley, they would get out of the car, looking behind dumpsters and trash cans, calling for Emily. Within hours, Layla was drooping and Maria had to reluctantly give up. She'd gone back to the volunteers' table to let them know, and then left for home.

Now Layla was safely sleeping in her bed.

Maria's mind raced, a jumble of questions that had no answers. Her heart broke for Emily's parents. The terror, panic, and helplessness of having a child missing was not lost on her. Nothing could compare to the agony—except, of course, not finding them alive.

God had blessed her. Layla was still alive.

Repeatedly Maria mentally ran through the day, always ended up at the same moment. The moment when she and Layla were walking back into the flower shop. She'd caught a flash of movement in her peripheral vision, but when she'd turned the street was empty.

Was that the moment someone grabbed Emily?

Her heart told her it was.

She hadn't mentioned the lurking man to the officers, since he wasn't there when Layla and Emily came home from school. Maybe she—

The phone rang. Maybe, they'd found Emily. But phone calls this late always meant bad news.

She bit her lip, not wanting to answer it. She picked up the phone and looked at the screen.

The call was forwarded from the flower shop and not her personal number.

Her muscles relaxed. Probably a customer. A husband panicked because he'd forgotten his wife's birthday or their anniversary. Or someone eloping and wanting a bouquet.

She always did what she could to help them out. Her success came from one satisfied customer at a time.

"Hello."

"Hello, Maria." The deep accented voice reached out from the grave.

The room spun as she fought to breathe. She wasn't hallucinating. This was real.

"You must have the wrong number." Her voice sounded steady, despite the chaos in her heart.

The caller laughed. "I don't think so, Maria, but I'll

give you an A for effort."

It was futile, but she continued the game. "Like I said, wrong number." She hit the disconnect button and was already moving towards Layla's room when the phone rang again. Her hand gripped the phone. This was crazy—impossible—and yet it was ringing.

She let it ring.

Her feet moved on their own accord to the kitchen. She pulled up a chair to the refrigerator and climbed atop it. Her hands fumbled until she found what she wanted. The gun safe.

The phone continued to ring.

Her hands shook as she hit the buttons on the electronic gun safe. Layla's birthdate—her real birthdate. The light flashed green. Maria lifted the lid and stared.

The phone stopped. The house returned to a deadly silence.

Her ragged breathing was the only sound.

Maria closed her eyes for a moment, but then opened them. One thing she'd learn through dealing with Raymond—stay in the real world. It was the only way to keep her daughter safe. Her heart trembled more than her hands as she lifted the gun out of the box.

For Layla, Maria would and could do what she had to.

The phone rang once again. This time she answered.

"Hello." She had to know if she and Layla needed to run again.

"Don't hang up again, Maria. Or you will regret it. Understand?" Anger tinged his words.

She nodded as she walked back into the living

room.

"I said, do you understand?"

"I understand." Her voice was a whisper.

"Good. Don't make me angry. You remember how I get when I'm angry, don't you?"

"I remember." Her eyes filled with tears. *Only too well.*

"Good. Let's act like civilized people and talk this through."

Except he wasn't civilized.

"You know what I want, right?"

She didn't think she could breathe, let alone answer. Her voice was a whisper. "No."

A cruel chuckle. "Of course, you know. Don't play games with me. Say her name, Maria. I want to hear you say it."

Closing her eyes, she hoped she wouldn't pass out. In spite of the dryness of her mouth, she managed to mutter her daughter's name. "Layla."

"See how easy that was. Now, you give me what I want and I'll release Emily"

Her legs wouldn't hold her up any longer. She stumbled back to the sofa. "Emily?" She'd known he was evil, but this was craziness. Why would he take Emily?

"That's right. Layla's little friend who's missing. You do know about that, don't you? She'll be released unharmed as long as you bring me what I want. My daughter. And then you can get on with your own little life."

Trade Emily for Layla?

"I won't have a life without Layla."

"Not my problem." He laughed.

She heard the familiar cruelty in it. *This couldn't be*

happening.

"And don't even think about calling the authorities. As long as you do what I tell you, everybody gets to live. Layla, Emily, and you."

"I don't believe you."

"Oh, I thought about killing you, believe me. But then your suffering would be over. I want you to live a long, long life...without Layla. That will be punishment enough for what you did to me, don't you think?"

"I won't do it."

"Why not? It's a win-win situation. Layla will have a wonderful life. A righteous life. A life of privilege. You will be doing her a favor to let her live the life she was born to live." A pause. "And Emily will get to go home to her own family."

"I won't do it."

"Of course, you will. You don't want Emily to die, do you? Can you live with that? Charge up your phone. I'd hate for it to go dead, just when you need it the most. I'll be in touch." Another pause. "If you don't answer I will kill the little girl. Make no mistake about that. I want Layla and I get what I want. You wouldn't want me to hurt Emily, would you?"

The phone went quiet.

She stood there holding the phone in one hand and her gun in the other.

Raymond. It wasn't possible. He was dead.

But her ex-husband was alive and ready for revenge.

She wouldn't let him have Layla. But how could she save Emily?

If she thought going to him would keep Emily safe, she would consider it—to keep Emily alive. But she knew he would kill her and Emily, and then disappear forever with Layla. The man was a monster, a liar, and a terrorist. And according to the FBI–dead.

They'd lied, too.

No one could help her.

7

On shaky legs, Maria rushed to the window and peered into the darkness.

The monster was out there, watching and waiting, ready to steal Layla.

Maria'd been naïve before, but no longer. How could she take Layla away without Raymond catching them?

Her mind froze.

Panic bubbled. Her breathing turned ragged, and she was on the verge of a panic attack.

None of this made any sense. Why not just take Layla that afternoon when he had the chance, rather than Emily?

Kidnapping Emily had been a mistake. And Raymond didn't make mistakes. Maybe he didn't have Emily at all.

Raymond. Alive.

Somewhere deep inside, she'd always known. She'd never felt safe. Her heart knew Raymond wasn't dead. And if he was alive, why was he a free man?

She forced her breathing to slow, but her mind worked overtime. She should call her contact at Witness Protection. But, they'd lied to her. She couldn't trust them. She couldn't trust anyone.

The FBI, Homeland Security. They told her Raymond was dead. And now, someone had betrayed her. Someone told Raymond her location.

No, she wouldn't call Morgan Reed. Even though she certainly hadn't told Raymond their location, just hours ago she'd refused to help. Morgan acted as if Maria was crazy, soothing her like a child, offering psychological help.

Maria couldn't trust anybody.

Except...Patti. Surely, Maria could trust her. Patti saved her life and rescued Layla. But Patti claimed she'd seen Raymond shot dead.

Had Patti lied?

Rejecting the idea, Maria shook her head. She couldn't believe Patti would lie, not after what they'd been through together. The authorities must have lied to Patti, as well. It was the only explanation.

Maria trusted Patti with her life—and with Layla's. If she could make it to Florida, Patti would keep Layla safe. Then, Maria could come back and tell the authorities about Raymond and Emily. She'd have to bluff him—make him think he was getting Layla, so he wouldn't hurt Emily—but she definitely couldn't go to the police until Layla was safe.

Maria walked into the kitchen. Wedging herself between the wall and the refrigerator, she pushed, and then grabbed the backpacks hidden behind it. She'd never quite trusted the fact she and Layla were truly safe. The escape bags were her backup plan. Always packed and ready to go in an instant.

One contained clothes and other necessities for Layla and herself. And the other contained all that remained of her old life—photos, birth certificates; and other valuable papers. She'd refused to get rid of them when she'd entered Witness Protection.

It also contained hope for a new life and money— lots of it. Raymond hadn't left them destitute—Witness

Protection made sure she received the money. She'd cashed the check and hidden the money with the bags.

For a rainy day.

And the rain was about to commence.

She walked back into the living room and stared out the window. Raymond was out there somewhere. If he could find the Flower Bouquet, he could find where she lived. He could be out there right this moment waiting for her to make a run for it.

He would be expecting her to drive away.

All she owned was the flower shop's van—too obvious.

Raymond was probably sitting in it waiting for them to run.

She had to get a different car, but how? Steal a car? She wouldn't know how—not that she could bring herself to steal a car. What a ridiculous thought.

She looked at her watch. It wasn't that late.

Surely, one of her neighbors would still be up. Maybe she could borrow a car. Might as well start with Mrs. Lytle—no, too nosy. She'd try the guy down the hall. She didn't know his name, but they always said hi when they saw each other.

At the end of the hall, she knocked and waited. Nothing. She knocked again—louder. After a moment, she heard movement, and then the door opened.

"I'm your neighbor down the hall." She pointed towards her apartment.

"Yeah, I know." His eyes were red and glassy. The smell of marijuana wafted out.

"I've got an emergency and I need to get to the airport, but my van's not working. I thought maybe I could borrow your car, and then you could take a cab to pick it up tomorrow." She held out a one hundred dollar bill. "I'll pay you for the cab ride and the inconvenience."

The door opened wider. "Make it two and I'll drive you up myself."

"My daughter's going with me and she gets upset around strangers. I need to drive myself."

"Glad to do it for five."

"That's ridiculous."

He shrugged, pushing his greasy brown hair out of his eyes. "I know, but we wouldn't want your daughter to get upset, would we?"

She gritted her teeth and smiled. "Fine. Thanks for being such a good neighbor."

"My car's in slot 215. Don't worry about the keys, just lock it up. I'll give you my spare and take mine with me to get the car."

She held out her hand for the key.

He held out his hand. "Where's my money?"

8

Her neighbor parked his car in the underground parking garage. A fortunate break for her. All she had to do now was wake Layla, and they'd be off. She dreaded having to tell her daughter they were leaving their home—again.

She picked up her purse, grabbed her cell phone, and then set it back on the coffee table.

Raymond had the number. He could track her movements. Better to leave it, but he'd said if she didn't answer the phone, he'd kill Emily.

Guilt pricked at her. She should stay and tell the police about the phone call from Raymond, but she couldn't risk Layla's life. Once Layla was safe in Florida, Maria would come back and help. In the meantime, she wouldn't risk Emily's life. As much as she hated doing it, she picked up the phone.

She walked into Layla's bedroom. Her little girl looked so peaceful, so sweet, so beautiful. Maria knew another move in the middle of the night would shatter her peace—maybe for good—but she had no choice.

"Layla, wake up. We have to go."

Her daughter murmured, but didn't wake up. Oh, well. No reason to wake her up. She picked her up. As she did Layla's stuffed giraffe fell out of the bed.

A gift from her father. Layla slept with it every night.

Maria bent down to pick up the giraffe, and then

stopped.

Layla needed to forget about her father.

Forget the giraffe…forget the monster.

****

Layla was buckled into the back of the car, still asleep. Their escape bags were in the trunk; it was time to go. Her hand shook as she put the key in the ignition.

If Raymond was watching, he would only see a woman driving away, not a woman and a child. And hopefully, because it was dark and she was in an unfamiliar vehicle, he wouldn't recognize her. Gone was the docile housewife whom Raymond had tricked, controlled, and manipulated.

In her place was Veronica Minor, a woman who would do anything to keep her daughter safe from monsters like him.

She glanced over her shoulder at her sleeping daughter. *Stay asleep, Layla. No reason for the nightmare to start sooner than necessary.*

If she could just get out of the parking lot, they'd be safe. She started the car, and then picked up the garage door opener. The parking spaces were empty of people.

She stopped at the closed garage door and lowered her eyelids.

God, I need Your help again. Please keep Layla far from the monster who is her father. Please keep us safe and keep Emily safe. Don't let him hurt her. In Jesus's name, amen.

Maria opened her eyes and hit the remote control.

The big door slid open. She drove out of the garage and into the darkness, leaving the protection of her home, but not God's protection.

He was more than enough.

She drove through the darkened parking lot, thankful for the light thrown from the pole lights. Her gaze flitted from one spot to another, but all was quiet. No one was lurking. But then again, Raymond knew how to hide. He'd kept his real identity a secret from her for years.

She approached the exit and turned left. She held her breath, waiting for another car to follow, her gaze glued to the rearview mirror.

Nothing. No car. No people.

She'd done it. She'd gotten away. Her muscles relaxed. She'd escaped—again.

As she drove, she mapped out the next move. She would buy tickets for the next flight out under the names of Veronica and Jasmine Minor. The destination didn't matter.

If Raymond checked the airlines, he'd find her—or so he'd think.

An hour later, she pulled into the airport, but instead of going to the terminal as originally planned, she stopped at the first car rental place. A glance in the backseat showed Layla was still asleep. Maria stepped out of the car and walked into the building. The place was deserted this time of the night, but the sign boasted it was open twenty-four hours a day.

"Hi." The rental agent looked up from the computer and smiled.

"I need a rental car."

He arched an eyebrow at her. "Sorta figured that."

"I suppose you did." A little flirting couldn't hurt. She tossed her head and smiled at him.

"I have a little problem. I borrowed a friend's car

to get here. He's going to pick it up, but I told him it would be in the long-term parking lot. Do you think you could drive it over for me?" She didn't flutter her eyelashes at him, but came close.

"I suppose I could do it on my break."

"Promise?" She winked at him.

His cheeks turned rosy pink as he nodded.

She handed him the keys. "Thanks so much. I'll be sure to stop in and say hi the next time I'm in the area."

"Promise?"

Feeling ridiculous, she winked. "Promise." She walked out and pulled out the escape bags, and then opened the back door. She couldn't carry Layla and the bags. Jostling Layla, she leaned in and whispered. "Come on, sweetie. We gotta go."

Her daughter's eyes opened. "Mommy, what...where are we?"

"It's OK. We gotta go."

"No, Mommy. I don't wanna go. I wanna sleep." Layla pulled away from her, not fully awake.

Maria unbuckled Layla, grabbed her hand and helped her out of the car. "Sorry, sweetie. We have to leave right now."

Layla whimpered as they walked to the rental. "Mommy. Where are we? What are we doing?"

"I'll explain it later."

Little sobs escaped from Layla as they walked to the rental car. Maria steeled her heart against reacting to them.

Once they were in the car and Layla was buckled into the back, Maria drove off. At the highway exit, she turned south.

"Mommy, I don't understand." Layla whined from the back seat. "Where are we going? What are you doing?"

She hated telling Layla it was time to move—again. "I know you don't and I'm sorry for that. But we needed to leave. In a hurry."

"No. I want to go back. We have to look for Emily." Her daughter's voice turned stubborn.

"We did look for Emily, remember?"

"We have to look some more. We have to look until we find her." Her daughter's voice rose in pitch and intensity. "I want Emily. I want Daddy."

Maria hardened her heart. It was the only way to keep the guilt and panic from overwhelming her. It was the only way to keep Layla safe.

More troubles were on the horizon.

"Look, I'm sorry, sweetie, but—"

"Don't call me sweetie. I hate you. I hate you. You are so mean," she screamed from the backseat. "I don't want to go."

Maria's eyes filled with tears, but she didn't respond.

What could she say? As a mother, she wasn't that great. It was her job to provide a happy, safe environment. And she wasn't doing a good job at either one.

9

Conrad walked into the police station in the early hours of the morning. He'd gone home to take a shower and let his dog out. He felt as exhausted as Zink looked.

They'd passed the twelve-hour mark of Emily Most's abduction. As far as they could deduce, this was a stranger abduction—the worst kind—and there was a shorter window of time to bring the child home safely.

"Hey, Zink. You OK?"

"I'm fine. I wish everybody would stop asking me that." Her voice was snappish. "We have a job to do. Let's just stay focused on Emily Most."

"If you say so."

"I say so. Stop worrying about me."

"I'm not worrying." He handed her coffee and a bag. "I don't really like you enough to worry about you. No, sirree. Not me."

"Such a tough guy, aren't you?" She peeked in the bag and pulled out a croissant. "Bless you."

"No problem. You should go home and get some rest. You really do look exhausted."

"Sure. Sounds like a good idea." She rolled her eyes as she pulled off a piece of the croissant. "I'll get right on it."

"Not happening, huh?"

"Not until we find this little girl. Was BowWow happy to see you?" She popped the piece of pastry in her mouth.

"Ecstatic. And the shower made me feel like a new man. You ought to try it."

After swallowing the bite, she said, "I don't want to feel like a man—new, or old."

"Very funny. What's going on?"

"Every registered sex offender in the county has an alibi. I don't know what our next move should—"

The door buzzed announcing a visitor. Nick Johns—one of the part-time officers on the Sunberry force. "It's over."

Relief flooded through Conrad.

Zink stood up. "They found Emily?"

"No, they didn't find her, but the state police have taken the lead with the FBI here to support. They informed the chief a little while ago. Told him to get on with taking care of the other stuff in town."

"He must be fit to be tied," Conrad said.

"That's putting it mildly. They showed up at the Mosts' and told the chief—their turf, not ours. Basically told us to go home and stay out of their way."

"You've got to be kidding. This is our town. We know it and the people better than anyone. I don't get why everyone is so territorial." Conrad thought they'd have a day or two before the turf wars started.

"Yeah, why can't we all just get along?" Zink chimed in.

"You don't have to tell me. I agree. What a mess. There's a lot of panic out there."

"And rightfully so." Zink stood and stretched. "Ever worked any kidnappings in the big city, Nick?"

"A few, but they were actually custody battles.

Stranger abductions are a whole different thing. In parental abd—" Nick stopped and stared at Zink. His dark complexion mottled red. He shrugged. "Well, you know. I don't have to tell you."

Conrad stared at the two of them. The look on Zink's face told him what he needed to know. Time to change the topic. Zink was in no mood to be coddled. He better intervene.

"I know they're the experts, but that doesn't mean we can't be helpful." Conrad broke the tense silence. "They shouldn't shut us out of the case."

Nick stifled a yawn. "And yet they are."

"I am not going to sit here and pretend she's not missing and act like it's just another day in Sunberry," Zink said. "We have to do something."

"According to the state police, that's exactly what we're supposed to do." Nick grabbed his time card, slipped it in, and then turned back. "So, I'm going home to bed. My shift's over."

"You're kidding, right?" Zink's mouth fell open.

"Nope. See you later." He walked out of the station.

"Close your mouth, Zink." Conrad told her.

"That man needs to be fired. He's worthless. We have a missing child and he goes home at the end of his shift."

"You should talk to the chief about that. He listens to you."

"He listens to you, too."

"Not the way he does to you. Back to the case. Any of those predators give you a hinky feeling?"

"They all did." She shuddered. "So creepy."

"That's for sure."

She tore off another bite of the croissant. After

swallowing, she looked at him. "I was thinking."

"That can't be good, but go ahead and tell me." He winked and gave an exaggerated sigh.

"Remember the little girl and her mom we talked with at the flower store?"

"Sure. Jasmine and Veronica Minor."

"I got the feeling the little girl was hiding something when we were gathering up that bouquet while you talked with her mom. I asked her some questions and she outright avoided answering them." Zink pointed to the bright colored flowers decorating her desk as if he'd forgotten the interview.

"About Emily?"

"I'm not sure, but I asked where they used to live and things like that. Just making conversation. And she seemed very evasive."

"How evasive can a first-grader be?"

"I get your point, but something was off. And they were the last people to see Emily. I think we should go back and talk with them again. Then, we can take a second look at the pervs."

"You aren't thinking they have something to do with Emily missing, are you?"

"Not really, but...something's off."

"I'm sure she doesn't know anything. The woman's just trying to raise her daughter alone. It's got to be tough. She probably told Jasmine not to tell people about their past. No big deal."

"A little defensive, aren't you?" Zink arched an eyebrow at him.

"Not at all. I'm just saying it's probably a waste of time." He grabbed the keys off his desk. "But let's go check it out, anyway. It's not a problem."

"I didn't think it would be a problem. I thought

you might want to see the mother again. Couldn't help but notice the way you looked at her."

"I have no idea what you're talking about, Zink."

"Sure you don't." She stood, grabbed another croissant and the coffee, and headed out.

****

Maria stared at the ceiling of their motel room. Her mind wouldn't function. It was as if she was in suspended animation—aware, but not able to move.

Raymond was alive.

The words kept running through her head, over and over like a broken record, along with the haunting sound of his voice and that cruel laugh.

The man had shot her three times, but she'd survived. With God's help, she'd survive this.

Why wasn't he in prison? How could the U.S. government—her government—leave an avowed terrorist and murderer to roam the streets?

He hadn't called back yet. She hoped she would be in Florida with Patti before he did.

She had no idea how organized Raymond's group was, or what they were able to do, but she wasn't taking any chances. All transactions would be cash so they couldn't track her by her credit card.

Unfortunately, there was still the matter of the cell phone, but it was turned off. He couldn't track her unless it was on. At least that's what the TV shows said. Eventually, she'd have to turn it on and deal with him.

But not yet.

The FBI had told her Raymond's terrorist cell had been decimated, but then again, they'd also told her

Raymond was dead. She had to remember she couldn't trust anything the authorities had said.

10

Conrad stood in front of the flower store, staring at the closed sign on the door.

"Why would she be closed?" Zink asked. "The sign says they should be open."

"Don't ask me. I just got here. There could be any number of reasons."

"My radar's going off." She moved closer to the window and peered in.

"Oh, no. The dreaded radar."

"You aren't making fun of my radar, are you? Because the radar works."

"Not at all. I respect your radar." He held his hands up in mock surrender. "Can your radar tell me where she is right now?"

"It's radar—not a GPS."

"That's what I thought. Let's see if we can find a home address. She might not be open because her daughter was upset and they've decided to continue looking for Emily."

"It's possible, but that's not what my radar is saying. Something suspicious is going on."

"What is it about this woman that you don't like?"

"Something is hinky about her. Like the way she made me show her my ID. Who does that in this town?"

"She's new to this town, and she's being careful. Nothing wrong with that."

"Really? Why don't you just admit you think she's pretty?"

He ignored her and walked back to the cruiser.

Zink jogged past him. She was already typing the name on the laptop mounted on the console between them as Conrad slid into the driver's side.

"No home phone listing. Something else suspicious."

"That is not suspicious, and you know it." He shrugged. "A lot of people are doing away with home phones. Who needs 'em? We all have cell phones."

"You just don't want to admit there could be a problem with the pretty flower lady." She snapped her seatbelt in place.

"That's ridiculous. I barely know the woman."

"You had coffee with her last week. Now I know why you've been buying flowers for your mother every week since she opened up the place."

It was true. He did find Maria attractive, but he certainly wouldn't admit that to Zink. Especially now that she seemed to be on a crusade against the woman.

"Any other ideas on how to get her address?" he asked.

"Her kid goes to school, so they'll have her address."

"Good idea, partner. I knew there was a reason I keep you around."

"You keep me around? Let's not get confused who has the seniority in this car." She laughed and followed his gaze back to the flower store.

A dark-haired man now stood in front of it, not moving, as if mesmerized by the flowers.

"What do you suppose he wants?" Zink asked.

The man moved closer to the door and peeked

inside.

"Flowers, I would imagine."

"You're so witty, Conrad Travis."

"I try my best to keep you entertained."

"My radar's beeping. Do you recognize him?"

"Nope." He put the cruiser back into park. "Mine is, too." He stepped out of the car.

The man was so intent on the flower shop that he didn't notice Conrad, at first.

The movement apparently broke his trance. His eyes widened as he took in Conrad's uniform. He turned to leave.

"Hold up a minute, sir." Conrad's voice echoed through the empty street.

The man's body language screamed wariness and he tensed, as if to run.

The moment passed as he relaxed so quickly that Conrad thought he'd imagined it.

The stranger stared at Conrad. "Yes."

"Did you need some help?" Conrad asked.

"Not at all, officer. I wanted to buy some flowers for my wife, but the place is closed even though the posted hours say she should be open. I was trying to see in—see if maybe she was in there and forgot to unlock the door."

"Used the shop before, have you?"

"No, just passing through town. I actually live in Circleville. I thought my wife deserved some flowers."

The guy didn't look old enough to have a wife. He looked more like a college student. Then again, Conrad was getting at that age where everyone looked like a kid to him. "How did you know a woman owned it?"

"Call me sexist." He smiled. "My wife does—all the time." He looked back at the flower store. "I guess she's not opening. The flowers will have to wait for another time. If we are finished?" he asked.

Conrad nodded and went to the cruiser.

The man got in his car and started to drive off.

"Something odd about that man," Conrad said to Zink.

She smiled and held up her cell phone. "I took his picture and..." She snapped another picture as they drove past his vehicle. "...and a picture of his car."

"And the license plate?"

She turned the phone in his direction. "Clear as day."

They drove to the school as Zink uploaded information to the computer.

"I'll go get the address and you can check out that license plate." Conrad stepped out of the car and jogged towards the school. In ten minutes, he was back.

Zink looked over at him as he slid into the driver's seat. "The car's a rental. He rented it early this morning at the airport. His name is David Hamm. According to his New York license, he's a resident of New York City."

"Mmm. He told me he lived in Circleville. Said he just arrived in town early this morning."

Zink pointed a finger at him. "Why would he lie about living around here? And why was he at the flower shop at all?"

"I don't know," he said. "But it might be worth checking."

"Speaking of The Bouquet, did you get an address for the pretty flower lady?"

"You think she's pretty? I hadn't noticed."

"Of course, you didn't."

"Stop playing matchmaker, Zink. I'm perfectly content with my marital status." He winked at her. "It took a little charm, but Mrs. Davenport finally let me take a peek."

Six minutes later, they pulled into the parking lot of Sunberry's one and only high rise apartment building.

After knocking several times on Veronica Minor's door, Zink pulled out her cell phone. "Might as well call the chief and see what's going on with the search."

"Good idea. I'm going to see if I can find a neighbor or two." Conrad went to the next door and knocked. A moment later, the door opened. He held out his ID before the woman could ask. "Hi, I'm Officer Conrad Travis. We're trying to reach Mrs. Minor, but she's not at her flower store and not here. Have you seen her today?"

The woman pointed at the end of the hall. "You might ask the man in two-fifteen. I saw her talking to him late last night. Way too late. Shameless, I say. I can just imagine what the two of them..." She held up a hand. "I'm not getting involved in it, but the man's a bit too young for her, if you ask me."

"Thanks." Conrad took a step back, but the woman moved towards him.

"Her and that daughter of hers move in and act like they're too good to talk to the rest of us. Every time I've tried to be friendly, she just waves and shuts the door."

"Thank you very much for your help. We need to go to talk to him." Zink chimed in as she grabbed Conrad's arm. "We better talk with him right now, partner." She headed towards the other end of the hall.

"Thanks for the rescue," he said in low tones.

"You're very welcome. What are partners for?" She knocked on the door of 215, and a few seconds later it opened.

A young man poked his head out. His hair was disheveled, and it looked as if he hadn't shaved—or bathed—in a few days.

"Yeah."

Conrad held up his badge in case the kid didn't notice the uniform. "I was looking for your neighbor— Veronica Minor. Do you—"

"Of course, you are. I knew it was too good to be true." The man closed his eyes and shook his head.

"What was too good to be true?" Zink stepped up.

The guy opened the door further. "You might as well come in. You're probably going to have a few questions for me and...I need to report a stolen car."

11

"Mommy."

Maria opened her eyes, surprised she'd actually fallen asleep. "Yes, Layla?"

"Do you still love me?" Her daughter stared at her with worried eyes.

"Of course, I love you. What sort of a question is that to ask?"

"Are you mad at me?"

"Why would I be mad at you, sweetie?"

"Cause I told you I hate you."

"Did you mean it?" She scooped Layla closer.

"No, but I shouldn't have said it. It was mean."

"It was mean, and you shouldn't have said it, but I love you, anyway. And I will always love you, no matter how mean you are to me. That's just the way mommies are."

"Why did we have to leave Sunberry? It was a nice place."

Her daughter was right. Sunberry was a nice place.

"It was time to move. I've explained it to you before. We can't live anywhere too long."

"Because of the bad men?"

Her heart lurched.

Layla shouldn't know there was so much evil out in the world. But it was a part of their life and the only way to keep Layla safe was for her know that evil existed.

"Yep, because of the bad men."

"I thought they couldn't find us anymore."

"I thought so too, but even mommies can be wrong."

And Witness Protection.

"But Daddy's angel can protect us. We should go back. Daddy's angel is probably looking for us. Daddy sent him to help us. I know he did."

Ah—the innocence of a child. Maria hoped she'd never have to tell Layla the truth about what kind of a monster her father really was.

"Angels can find us wherever we are."

"Really?"

Maria nodded, hoping this particular angel never found them again.

"I'm worried about Emily. Do you think they found her yet? Can we call and see if she came home?"

"I'm worried about her, too, but we can't call. I'll figure out a way for you to call later. OK?"

"Did the bad men take Emily, Mommy?"

"I don't know." Raymond claimed he'd taken Emily and Maria was acting on that assumption, but logic said he had nothing to do with kidnapping Emily. He was just using the girl's disappearance for his own gain. It didn't make sense that he'd snatch Emily when Layla was right there, too.

"But they might have?" Layla sat up in bed, waiting for an answer.

"Yes, they might have."

"Then you have to tell the police, Mommy. If you tell them about the bad men, they'll be able to find Emily, right?"

Shards of guilt pricked her conscience. "Not

necessarily, sweetie. I have to take you somewhere safe first then I'll do exactly that. "

"But, Mommy—"

"No buts, Layla," Maria said. "It's my job to keep you safe. And that's what I'm going to do."

"What about Emily, Mommy? Don't you want to keep her safe?"

****

Conrad exchanged a look with Zink as they listened to Ricky Snyder.

It couldn't be coincidental that Veronica had left the same day as Emily's kidnapping. Why hadn't she taken her own vehicle? Could she be one of those women who kidnapped children because she couldn't have her own? Maybe Jasmine was a kidnap victim, as well.

Zink's radar was working much better than his own.

He'd been too enamored with Veronica Minor and those big dark eyes. His mind flashed back to their conversation about secrets. She hadn't actually said she didn't have any. He should have asked more questions.

And now she'd fled during the night.

With Emily?

Was it possible Emily was in that flower store the whole time they were talking to Veronica? The three croissants and juice churned in his stomach. If that was the case, he should give up police work—he had no right to wear a badge.

"So, you don't really know if she stole your car since you didn't actually go up to the airport, yet,"

Zink asked.

The young man slouched on his sofa, but nodded vigorously, his greasy hair bobbing. "Yeah, that's true. But I figure if you're looking for her, she probably needed a car y'all wouldn't be looking for. So...there you have it."

Zink looked at Conrad and shook her head as if to say *I told you so*. "I'm going to call airport security and have them check the parking lots." She stood up, holding the paper she'd written the information on. "I'll let you know what I find."

"So, how many kids did you see her with last night?" Conrad asked.

"Just the one, but I didn't go down to the car with her. You think she stole that little girl I heard about on the news?"

"Was it her daughter?"

"Couldn't really tell. The kid was asleep and her face was hidden."

Asleep or drugged?

There was nothing else to learn here. But he'd sure like to take a look in Veronica's apartment. He didn't have enough for a search warrant, yet.

Conrad looked down at the coffee table. "And the next time you invite police into your apartment." He leaned down and picked up the baggie and tossed it on the man's coffee table. "I suggest you put your stash away." Conrad had already judged it to be less than an ounce, so he couldn't bust the kid for anything more than a misdemeanor.

Ricky Snyder's mouth fell open. "Uh...it's not mine."

Conrad met his gaze. "Good, then you won't mind if I take it to dispose of it?"

Ricky's nose twitched and his face turned red. "Uh...no...of course not. I don't even know how it got there. One of my buddies must have dropped it. I don't do that stuff."

Sure he didn't.

Zink turned away so the kid wouldn't see her smiling, but not before Conrad saw. "We'll let you know about your car, Mr. Snyder," Zink said.

"Uh—OK, thanks."

"No, thank you for all your cooperation." Conrad held up the baggie. "Especially for this. We wouldn't want this to get in the wrong hands, would we?"

"Uh...no, sir."

Conrad stared hard at the young man. "Look, I know you think everyone does this stuff, but you do know this isn't good for your brain, right?"

Ricky nodded.

"I'm giving you a break this time, but you better clean up your act. Next time, I won't be so lenient."

They walked out and down the hall.

"Think he's watching out of his peep hole?" Zink asked.

"Without a doubt. He wasn't the brightest bulb in the pack, was he?" Conrad motioned towards Veronica Minor's door. "I'd sure like to get into that apartment. It could tell us a lot about where she went and why she left in such a hurry."

Zink nodded. "Good idea, but we don't have a reason to ask for a warrant. Although, it wouldn't hurt to ask the manager, I suppose."

He slipped the baggie in his pocket. "I don't want to walk around with that. Let's go find the manager."

They found a door marked "Manager" and knocked. The salty smell of bacon made Conrad's mouth water.

"Hi, can I help you?" A young woman smiled at them. "Are you looking for something to rent?"

He pulled out his badge. "No. I was hoping to take a look at someone's apartment, but they're not answering. Think you could let me take a look?"

Her eyes widened, and she twisted a lock of hair. "Why? Who?" She glanced over her shoulder, and then back at them. "Hold on, I need to shut off the bacon before it burns. Be right back."

True to her word, she was back in a moment. "Who's apartment?"

Zink stepped in front of him with an easy smile. "Veronica Minor. She didn't open up the flower shop this morning, and we wanted to make sure she was all right."

"Gosh, I don't know. This has never happened before. I'm not sure if I'm allowed to do that or not. I usually just collect the rent."

"Do you have someone you want to call and ask?"

"Uhm...no...I don't see why you can't go check on her. Hold on a minute, let me get the keys for you." The door closed.

"That was easier than I expected." Zink smiled.

"It was." He agreed.

The door opened and the young woman handed Zink the keys. "You don't need me to go with you, do you? I got a baby and I'm cooking breakfast."

"No need at all." Zink gave her a bright smile.

12

Conrad unlocked the door and held it open for Zink.

"What a gentleman. Any woman would be pleased to have you. Even the pretty flower lady."

"Not likely, now that we're breaking into her house."

"We are not breaking in. We have permission."

"I doubt if Veronica will see it that way—or a judge, for that matter." He stepped inside the apartment and closed the door. The apartment had a barren, empty feeling.

"Probable cause, partner. The guy down the hall says she stole his car."

"Sure, Zink. Sure. If you're expecting us to find the car in the living room."

"Besides, it's the truth. I am worried about her. My radar's going off again. Something isn't right."

"I agree, but I'm not sure it has anything to do with Emily Most."

"Why would she and her kid disappear at the same time as Emily? Not a flair for home decor, considering the woman owns a flower shop," Zink said. "No family pictures. Nothing homey here."

"I was thinking the same thing."

"Almost as if she didn't expect to be here all that long."

Words defending Veronica jumped to his mind,

but he kept them off his lips.

Zink was right, as much as he hated to admit it. He moved out into the kitchen. "This is odd."

"What's that?" Zink's voice carried from the other room.

"Come and see."

The refrigerator had been shoved away from the wall. A small door behind it hung open. He knelt down and peered inside. It was too dark to see anything.

"Did you move that?" Zink asked.

"Nope. It was already like that." He pulled out his flashlight and peered into the tiny cubicle. "It's empty."

Zink's fingers tapped against each other—a sure sign her mind was working overtime. "What do you think?"

"I'm thinking Veronica Minor had something important she needed to hide. Wonder what it was." He dusted off his pants as he stood. Not that the floor was dirty. In fact, it was immaculate. He'd hate to see what the floor looked like behind his refrigerator. Probably time to clean it—one of these days. "Find anything else?"

"As a matter of fact, I did. Their luggage."

"And..."

"And if she was going on a trip, why wouldn't they pack clothes? Checked their drawers. It didn't look as if anything was gone."

"Maybe she kept extra suitcases in there." He pointed at the cubicle.

"Yeah, maybe." Zink shrugged. "And another thing. I went through her desk and couldn't find an address book or a list of phone numbers. Nothing personal. Nothing that indicated she had plane reservations, either."

"Maybe, she didn't. Ricky said it was an emergency. So, maybe her plan was to go to the airport and fly standby."

"With a child?"

"It's possible."

"It's also possible she lied to Ricky."

****

In the cruiser, Zink called the airport. It took three people, but she finally found the right person. After she hung up, she looked over at Conrad. "Security's checking the lots for his car. So, what are you thinking?"

He slipped the key into the ignition. "If they find the car, then maybe she had a legitimate emergency like she told him, and it was simply a coincidence that it happened on the day Emily went missing. Not everything is part of a conspiracy, you know."

"And if they don't find his car?"

He started the car and put it into gear before answering. "Could be a problem for Veronica Minor. Either way, I think we should go back to the station and see what we can find out about her."

13

Conrad walked into the station behind Zink. Other than the dispatcher, the place was empty. The others were probably out looking for Emily or running errands for the state police and the FBI.

Except for Nick Johns—he apparently was at home taking a nap. Conrad had no idea why Nick only worked part-time at his age. And he always seemed to have plenty of money

Something wrong with that scenario. Once this thing with Emily was resolved, he'd be having a talk with the chief if Zink didn't.

The police station was housed in the small municipal building and shared space with the mayor's office, the town council meeting room, and the town's maintenance department.

With a population of less than five thousand, they had six full-time officers, including the chief of police, and four part-time. The department was more than adequate until a major catastrophe occurred, like Emily Most's disappearance. The Sheriff's Department and the state police were called in for extra help.

"If I were a bank robber, today would be the day to rob every bank and store in town," Zink muttered.

"Isn't that the truth?" Conrad agreed. "Maybe that's what's going on. Maybe, it's an elaborate ruse to keep us busy while they rob the town blind."

"I wish." She sat at her desk and her fingers hit the

keyboard. "OK, let's see what we can find out about the pretty flower lady."

"I'll run an Internet search while you look at the official records."

Zink's phone rang. When she hung up, she winked at him. "Your girlfriend's in the clear. Apparently. Mr. Ricky Snyder's car is in the long-term parking lot waiting for him to come find it." She held up her phone. "I'll give him a call."

Ignoring her girlfriend comment, Conrad scrolled through various articles about Veronica Minor, but none of them were about their Veronica.

Zink walked to her desk and sat.

He formed a steeple with his fingers and tapped them together.

A few minutes later Zink clicked her phone shut, laughing.

"What's so funny?" Conrad lifted a coffee cup to his lips.

"Mr. Ricky Snyder wanted to know if I'd drive him to the airport to pick up his car. And when I told him I was a little busy hunting for Emily, he asked if I'd like to go out with him some time."

He laughed. "You could do worse."

"I have done worse. That's why I've given up dating for the time being. Find anything interesting?"

"In a way." He shook his head. "In fact, I've found nothing. For her, or the flower store. Seems odd that she wouldn't at least have a web page for the business."

"Very odd. Seems everybody has a web site these days." She hit the keyboard. A moment later, she looked up. "No arrests or convictions. The only thing I found was her license application with the Ohio DMV, but she only got it three months ago."

"That must have been about the time she moved to town."

"You should know. You're the one who's been buying flowers every week. I don't know why you don't just ask her out and be done with it."

"Contrary to what you believe, I am not on the prowl." He was glad to know that his instincts about Veronica Minor were right.

She was exactly what she said—a widow struggling to raise her daughter alone.

"Interesting. She came in and took the complete test rather than transferring a license from another state. I wonder where she lived before."

He shrugged. "The school should have a record of the daughter's previous school, right? I'll call. You keep digging."

Zink stared at him with her perfectly arched eyebrows when he hung up. "Well?"

"Evidently, Jasmine was homeschooled and had no records."

"Well, there should be some sort of records even if she was homeschooled."

"Apparently not. You'd think so, but maybe some states are more relaxed about homeschooling records than Ohio. Go figure."

She jumped up and marched towards the coffee pot. "Something's wrong with this woman. She's hiding something. I can feel it. My radar is shrieking at me."

Conrad shook his head. "That is not necessarily true. There could be plenty of legitimate reasons why we can't find any information on her."

She walked back and handed him a cup of coffee.

"And plenty of illegitimate reasons as well."

"All I'm saying is 'don't jump to conclusions.' I know—"

"Know what? You think a pretty woman can't do something illegal?"

"Don't be ridiculous. Of course, they can, but—"

"Things like this don't happen in Sunberry, Conrad. This is crazy." She slammed the cup on her desk and turned to him. "What is really going on here? It feels like our little town's falling apart."

"Unfortunately, there's a first time for everything, Zink. Forget about Veronica Minor for the moment. Let's stay focused on Emily."

Zink was getting herself worked up.

He'd seen it before. "It's important not to jump to conclusions too soon. It only hampers an investigation."

"That sounds like it came straight out of a textbook." She glared at him, and then started pacing again. "What if Jasmine isn't Veronica Minor's daughter at all, and now she's kidnapped a second girl. Emily might have been in the back of the flower shop the whole time we were there. Why didn't we check?"

"Because she wasn't a suspect then, and she's still not." His voice was firm. He'd been seeing Veronica Minor every week for the past few months at the flower shop. If she was a kidnapper, he'd have noticed something. She was a pretty woman who was fun to talk with, not a crazed kidnapper.

Zink ignored him. "And who knows? Maybe she only wants one daughter at a time and so it might be time to dump Jasmine. She might be in as much danger as Emily." She stopped pacing and set her coffee down on his desk. "I'm calling the chief."

Conrad stared at her and shook his head. "You jumped to a conclusion."

14

In spite of Layla's guilt trip, Maria drove towards Florida, sure she was doing the right thing. *And what about Emily?* The words resonated from somewhere in her spirit.

She did her best to ignore them. When it didn't work, she turned the radio up louder. She sang along, pretending this was a carefree road trip—not an escape.

Layla didn't sing along.

Exhaustion sneaked up on Maria once again, much sooner than expected. When her eyes drooped closed, she knew it was time to pull over and get a hotel room even though it was early. Falling asleep at the wheel wasn't something she wanted to risk.

They hadn't made good time, but at least they were farther away from Sunberry—and from Raymond.

She paid with cash and registered under one of her old aliases that she'd kept in her escape bag along with her real documents.

"Let's go swimming, Layla."

"I don't want to." Her daughter's tone was truculent.

"But you love to swim. It's why I picked this hotel. So you could go swimming in the indoor pool. We'll go buy a bathing—"

Her daughter shook her head, tears pooling in her

brown eyes. "No, Mommy. I don't want to go swimming. I want to go home and tell the police about the bad men. I want them to find Emily."

"Layla, the police are doing everything they can to find Emily. That's their job, and I'm sure they'll find her soon."

"But what about the rule, Mommy?"

Maria shook her head, knowing she didn't want to hear whatever Layla was about to say.

Layla persisted. "I thought the rule was we always help people if we can. I think we need to help Emily."

Her daughter stared up at her with trusting brown eyes, waiting for an answer.

****

Conrad stepped off the elevator and walked towards Ricky Snyder's apartment once again. The door opened. Ricky had obviously been watching for him.

Ricky stepped out of his apartment. His mouth formed a perfect O. Guess he hadn't been looking for Conrad. He'd been leaving, even after he'd called. "Going somewhere, Ricky?"

"Uh...yeah...I got me an appointment. I told the cop on the phone that."

"You called twenty minutes ago. I came as soon as you called."

"Why?"

"Why what?"

"Why did you come?"

"Because you called us and said you found something that might be important, so I came."

"I know that, but the other officer already came."

A knot formed in Conrad's stomach. "Who are you talking about?"

"He just left a few minutes ago. That's why I was leaving."

The knot tightened. "Tell me what happened." He hadn't told anyone else about Ricky's call, and no other officer should have showed up.

"I heard knocking and opened my door, but the man was knocking on her door." Ricky pointed at Veronica Minor's door. "I asked him if he was the cop you sent to talk with me and he said yes."

"Did he show you some identification—like maybe a badge?"

"No, he must have been a detective 'cause he wasn't wearing a uniform."

"We don't have any detectives in Sunberry, Ricky." It took all his patience not to add the word moron.

"Oh. Maybe, he was from the Sheriff's office."

"No detectives there, either. Never mind. What did you tell him?"

"I found a piece a paper in the car. It was from a car rental agency. I thought it was strange because I thought she was flying somewhere, but she rented a car at the airport. Wonder why she would do that?"

Strange indeed.

"What was the name of the rental agency?"

He shrugged. "It was on the paper. I don't remember."

Of course he didn't remember.

"Where's the slip?"

"The other guy took it."

Of course, he did.

"But it wasn't Veronica's name on the paper,

anyway. That's why I thought it might be important. Maybe someone else is with her. You know—like an accomplice."

That was interesting. "What was the name?"

Ricky's eyes widened, reminding him of a deer caught in the headlights. "Can't remember."

Conrad was losing his patience with this kid. "Look, Ricky. I'm not playing around here. You need to remember the name. It could be important. Lives could depend on it. Otherwise I might take you down to the station until you do remember."

Perspiration popped out on Ricky's forehead. "Oh, don't do that. I got places to go. Let me think a minute. It was...it started with an R."

"Rachel?"

He shook his head.

"Rayene? Rickie? Rona?"

"Ooh. Something like Rona." He snapped his fingers. "Ramona. That's it—Ramona Dye."

"Are you sure?" *Who was Ramona Dye?*

"Yep, I can see it clear as day."

As if he could see anything clear as day.

"What did this guy look like?"

"He was taller than me, dark complexion, but not African-American. Maybe Hispanic. He had an accent, but it didn't sound like Hispanic. His hair was black. Dressed nice."

Conrad's knotted stomach churned. It was the perfect description of the man from The Bouquet. He pulled out his cell phone and flipped through the pictures Zink had emailed to him.

He held it up to Ricky. "Is this the guy?"

"Yeah, that's him. Who is he?"

"Not a detective, that's for sure."

Zink's radar was right. Veronica Minor was involved.

15

"You are *not* going to believe this." Zink said the moment Conrad walked back into the station.

"Probably not, but try me." He stretched and tried to stifle a yawn. He failed. The caffeine was wearing off. He needed to get some sleep or he wouldn't be able to function.

"Ramona Dye and Veronica Minor are the same person. Ramona's Utah driver's license pic confirms it. Both came up with no known information under the criminal database." She looked at him with triumph in her eyes.

"Go ahead and say it."

"Say what?"

"That you were right and I was wrong. Something isn't right about the pretty flower lady."

"I would never gloat. At least, not much. Besides, we don't really know anything for sure yet. But something's going on. What else did you find out from Ricky?"

"That David Hamm was at Veronica's apartment." He went on to explain the mix-up.

"Mmm. Interesting. We know he didn't arrive until this morning, or at least that's when he rented the car. So the question is what's he got to do with all this?"

"I can't believe Veronica kidnapped Emily."

"You need to start thinking like a cop not a love-sick teenager. It's been a while since you've been in a relationship. Maybe you should get—"

"Don't go there, Zink."

She grinned. "Oh, that's right. I forgot you're an unmarried Christian and that means celibacy. Right?"

"My sex life, or lack thereof, is not up for discussion. The question is, who is Veronica Minor slash Ramona Dye or whatever name she's going by now, and did she have something to do with Emily's kidnapping. And why is David Hamm looking for her?"

"That's the question."

"So...what's the answer?"

Zink clicked her nails on the desk for several moments, and then looked up at him. "Maybe Veronica and David are a different story altogether. Maybe they don't have anything to do with Emily."

He forced his voice to be patient. "But it was your theory, Zink. Remember?"

"I know it was, but Jasmine seemed to be such a great kid. Bright and sweet. Kidnapped kids..." her voice trailed off.

He put a comforting hand on her shoulder. "Your radar must be on the fritz. Better call the repairman."

"I wonder how he just happened to show up at her apartment today of all days? And why did he lie to you and say he was from Circleville? Explain that to me."

He shrugged. "I can't. Why don't you see if you can find out anything about him? You've got his home address. See if you can find a home number and call him. Maybe check out the local hotels and see if he's staying in one."

She nodded and went to her desk.

Conrad went to his own computer and began cold

calling every car rental place in or near the Columbus airport. On the sixth call, he found the right place. When he finished, he looked over at Zink. "Good news and bad."

"Of course. Nothing's ever easy."

"The good news is she definitely rented a car. Bad news, no GPS or TrackTime."

"Then, it doesn't do us a whole lot of good."

"What did you find out about David Hamm?"

"Not much. No home phone, and according to Mapfind that address doesn't exist. And none of the hotels I've called so far have him registered."

"They gave you the info?"

She shrugged. "It helps to have grown up here. I know most of the people in one way or another. I still have a few more to try. "

"Mmm. Things get curiouser and curiouser, don't they, Officer Zink?"

The chief of police walked in, his face almost as red as his hair and mustache. "I'm sick of this. Those people act like we're idiots just because we work in a small town."

Ben Martin was normally easy-going, but he wasn't a happy camper at the moment. Conrad didn't blame him. Frustration gnawed at him, too. All he had was questions. He wanted some answers.

"What's the problem now?" Zink asked.

Conrad knew what she was doing—giving the chief time to vent. He obviously needed to.

"The head honcho from the state police suggested I should check for known sexual offenders in the area. As if we didn't do that within the first hour Emily was missing. They don't even want to use this place as their headquarters. They've set up at the State Patrol

Headquarters instead."

That was a slap in the face. Conrad knew the answer but asked the question anyway. "Have they found anything?"

"Nothing useful. They told me to go get some rest."

A nap was sounding better and better to him, but it would have to wait for a little while. Conrad walked over to Ben. "We might have a lead, but we aren't sure."

"Tell me about it."

"Veronica Minor, the woman who owns that flower shop, left town in a real hurry."

"And that makes you suspicious...why?"

"No, what makes us suspicious is she rented a car under an alias. And apparently lived under the alias in Utah until a few months ago when she moved in using the name Veronica Minor."

Ben arched a red brow at him. "That's something. Keep checking."

Suzanne walked over to them. "And she was the last person who saw Emily."

"And you think her own kid would lie for her?"

"It wouldn't be the first time." Conrad paused. "And we don't even know if Jasmine is really her child. We're having trouble finding any reliable information about either of them."

Ben looked over at Zink. "What do you think, Suzanne?"

"Something's going on with her. We just aren't sure if it has to do with Emily or something else."

"She doesn't fit the profile the FBI gave us. They think it's a man in his mid to late twenties."

"They've been wrong before."

"Yes, they have."

Ben Martin sighed. "You know, I never wanted this job."

Zink laughed. "You say that every time a real problem comes up."

"And I'm going to keep on saying it. OK, you can dig a little deeper but don't waste too much time on her. They're setting up another search. This time outside city limits, but I want us as a department to be there, too."

Zink looked at the chief. "Well, you might want to call Nick. He went home to take a nap."

Ben Martin's eyes narrowed. "A nap?"

"That's what he said. A nap."

The chief arched a bushy red brow. "Call him and the other part-timers. Tell them to be at the search this afternoon."

Zink nodded and walked back to her own desk.

Conrad nodded. "Then there's this other guy?"

"What other guy?"

"Well, it's not much, but we came across him today at the flower shop. He said he was from Circleville and wanted to buy flowers, but he lied. And he was at Veronica Minor's apartment." Conrad told the chief what they knew about David Hamm.

When Conrad finished, Zink looked over at them. "I just had a thought. Maybe this Hamm guy is Veronica's ex, and she's hiding from him. After Jasmine was on TV, she got worried about him seeing them and decided to leave."

"She said her husband died." Conrad pointed out.

"That would be the simplest way to hide from an abusive husband. That could also explain the aliases. And that would mean she didn't have anything to do with the kidnapping."

Conrad stared at her. "Maybe it's just me because I'm so tired, but you sure do seem to be flip-flopping about this woman."

"You're the one who told me not to jump to conclusions." She smiled sweetly. "I'm keeping an open mind."

"So was I. If you're right, she could be in danger, as well."

"When it rains, it pours," Ben said as he filled a cup with coffee.

Zink shook her head as she put the phone down." Nick's not answering his home or cell phone."

"Keep trying." Ben blew on the coffee and looked at Zink, his eyes probing. "Are you OK, Zink? If this is too much for you, you can let the rest of us handle it. There's no shame in it."

She shook her head. "I'm fine. I wish people would stop worrying about me. It's not the same at all, Ben. Just let me do my job and let me help bring Emily back to her parents."

The chief nodded, but he didn't look any more convinced than Conrad was.

16

Layla stared at her with those big brown eyes, waiting for an answer.

"You're right about the rule, Layla. And I'm going to help Emily, but first I have another rule I have to follow."

"What rule is that, Mommy?"

"It's the number one mommy rule."

A hint of a smile crossed Layla's face. "I never heard of that before."

"The number one mommy rule is that mommies are always, always, always supposed to protect their children, no matter what. So, I'm going to take you somewhere safe, and then I'm going to go help—"

The phone rang. *Raymond.*

She hadn't wanted to, but she'd turned it on a while ago. Afraid if she didn't, she would anger Raymond to the point he might hurt Emily.

She couldn't talk in front of Layla. Her daughter was too smart to be fooled. It would be awful if she figured out Maria was talking with her father. Her dead father.

Maria grabbed her phone. "Honey, I'm going to go in the hall and talk. Watch some TV until I come back."

"But, Mommy."

"Please, Layla. Don't make a fuss."

Layla nodded, but clearly was not happy. Once in the hall, Maria pressed the answer button. "Hello."

"You didn't listen to me. You shut the phone off and you left town. I told you there would be dire consequences for Emily if you did either."

"Did you really think I would just sit and wait for you to come and kidnap my daughter—again?" Her knees shook too badly to keep standing. She leaned against the wall and slid down onto the carpeted floor of the hallway. Her finger plucked at a loose loop in the carpet. "I'm not going to let you anywhere near my daughter."

"She is my daughter as well."

"Not anymore. You lost that right when you kidnapped her and shot me." She managed to keep her voice from shaking, whether from fear or fury she wasn't sure.

"I am her father. I will give you one more chance. I do not want to harm the pretty little Emily, but I will. You bring my daughter to me, and I will give you Emily back unharmed."

God, please keep Emily safe.

"How do I know you even have her?"

"If I didn't take her, then who did? Someone else in that hideous little town you live in? Did you really think you could hide from me? I will find you wherever you try to hide. It matters not what you do or don't do, I will always find you, Maria. Layla belongs to me, and I have a duty to raise her right."

"I was told you died."

He laughed. "Apparently I did not."

Stay focused. Keep the conversation about Emily. "If you have Emily, let me talk to her."

"Not going to happen. You will do what I say. Or trust me, you're going to regret it, and so will Emily. I will call you again. Be sure to answer."

The monster had kidnapped Emily, just the way he had Layla. Maria tried to block the memories, but couldn't.

****

It had started at the park.

Layla had giggled as she tumbled out of the car and tore across the grassy field. Maria followed behind at a slower pace. Layla loved the swings and it was always the first place she went.

A man walked up to Layla and squatted down to talk with her.

Maria ran across the park, yelling her daughter's name.

Layla and the man turned towards her.

He stared at Maria for a moment, stood, and then walked away.

By the time she reached Layla, the man was nowhere in sight. Her breathing was ragged as she asked, "What did that man say to you?"

"Nothing. He just said 'hi.'"

"He didn't ask you anything?"

"No." Layla ran to the swings and jumped on.

It was too hard to focus. Seeing the strange man talk to her daughter had scared her. Raymond's odd behavior and the strange man made her feel as if her world was crumbling.

When she left the park and returned home, the phone was ringing. Certain that it was Raymond, she took her time getting into the house. She didn't want to talk to him just yet, to tell him a strange man had managed to get close to Layla. He would be so infuriated; it was hard to know how he would react.

Pretending to be cheerful when she felt so vulnerable would be hard. It was her job to keep Layla safe.

Layla tugged at her mom's sleeve. "Mommy, hurry up. I have to go potty."

She slipped the key in the lock and opened the door.

The phone stopped ringing.

Maria expelled the air she'd been holding. As she walked into her kitchen, it didn't feel like home any longer. It felt like it belonged to a stranger.

The phone rang again.

Looking at the ID, she knew she had to answer. She took a deep breath and picked up the phone. "Hi, honey." She forced herself to sound normal.

"I've tried calling you several times today." His voice was angry—and accented.

"We just walked in from the park"

"And did she have a good time at the park?"

Did she detect a hint of smugness in his voice?

Should she tell him about the man watching them? Raymond might be able to protect Layla. He wouldn't let anything happen to his daughter, would he?

Her mind was jumbled. "Something happened."

"What?"

"Some man followed us."

Raymond chuckled.

Maria felt the rush of blood warm her face.

"Don't be ridiculous, Maria. I'm sure it was your imagination."

Again, Maria could hear an unmistakable accent. Usually, Raymond was overprotective of Layla. She'd expected him to be upset. "I'm not being ridiculous. I know what I know"

"He's probably just a father out for the day with

his child."

"He didn't have a child with him. He was following us. I'm sure of it."

"I doubt that very much, Maria." He chuckled once again. "Sometimes, you can be too protective of our daughter."

Maria refused to rise to his bait. "What would you like for dinner tonight?"

"Nothing."

Her heart skipped a beat. "Why? Are we going out to dinner?"

"Layla is going to spend the night with her little friend, Fiona. That way you can go shopping for a new dress tomorrow. I'm going to stay at the office and finish up some work. So, you have a free night."

Maria had trouble breathing.

Raymond had never allowed Layla to stay overnight anywhere before.

"That's not necessary. I don't need a new dress. I have plenty of dresses to choose from."

"You've worked very hard on this benefit and I want you to look beautiful. I insist upon it." The tone in Raymond's voice told her there would be no discussion about the matter. The accent was back.

What was going on here? Raymond wasn't acting like himself at all. The vague unease she'd felt since this morning turned into suspicion. Of what, she didn't know. The possibilities tumbled through her mind. This kind of thing only happened on television, not in real life. She was Maria Hammond, wife of Raymond, and they lived a happy life in the suburbs. The stranger in the park came to mind again.

Panic began to rise in Maria's chest. "No, Layla is tired. She's had a busy day. You know how cranky she can get when she's tired. I wouldn't want her to misbehave at their house."

"She will be fine," He was speaking in that odd cadence, again. "I will hear no more about it. Fiona is already expecting her so we wouldn't want to disappoint her. They will pick her up in about thirty minutes. Have an overnight bag ready for her. Then you go shopping, get your hair and nails done, and have a good time. I have a late meeting so I will see you when I get home."

He hung up.

It was time to leave. The fear rising in her heart had nothing to do with rational thought. Something was very wrong. Maria froze with indecision, but her mind raced from one crazy thought to another. Had she forgotten how to make decisions for herself?

She wasn't going to let him take Layla away from her. If he wanted a divorce and custody, she would fight him.

She and Layla needed to leave, but she couldn't think what to do first.

The doorbell snapped her out of her stupor.

Maria looked around the room, and then at her watch. It had only been two minutes, not a half hour. An icy calm fell over her. She walked to the door and opened it. "Oh, Renata. I'm sorry you made the trip over for nothing. I just got off the phone with Raymond. I don't think it's a good idea for Layla to go to your house today. We've had a busy day today, and Layla's tired and cranky. I'll just drop her tomorrow for a play date while I go shopping, if that's OK with you?"

"Oh, well. It's not like it's out of the way." She laughed, but her tone and expression indicated confusion.

"I know and it's so sweet of you to offer. I'll call you tomorrow."

"Are you sure? Because Raymond was quite insistent I take her so you could have the rest of the day to yourself since the big party's coming up." Renata stepped into the foyer without an invitation.

Maria didn't have time for idle chit-chat. She needed to get this woman out of her house so that she and Layla could leave. "Renata, this really isn't a good time. I don't mean to be rude, but I need to take care of Layla. Like I said, she's exhausted. I think she may be coming down with a cold."

Maria gently steered Renata out the door as she spoke. "Thanks so much for the offer to take Layla, but I'm going to have to say no this time."

Maria gave Renata a last gentle push and shut the door, being sure to lock it. Maria watched through the window as Renata walked slowly down the steps. At her car, she turned back and stared at the house, but she didn't leave.

Maria took a deep breath and made her decision.

She and her daughter were leaving right that second. If she was wrong then so be it, but her daughter's safety came first.

"Layla," Maria called as she walked back to her daughter's room.

"What, Mommy?"

"Come on. We're going to take a ride."

"Why? We just got home. Where are we going?"

"Mmmm. I don't know. Want to get some ice cream?"

"Yeah." Layla agreed with enthusiasm.

"Let's go."

"Just a minute." Layla started cleaning up the toys she'd been playing with.

Maria's nerves were a mess. Her first reaction was to yell and just grab Layla and get to the car, but she didn't want to scare her daughter. Forcing her voice to be calm, she took hold of Layla's hand. "We need to go now, sweetie. Hurry. We'll clean up when we get back."

That wouldn't be happening any time soon.

"But Daddy..."

"Don't worry about it." Maria pulled her daughter along and said playfully, "Come on. Come on. I want ice cream. I scream, you scream, we all scream for ice cream!"

Layla giggled.

As they passed the door, Maria glanced out the window. Her heart skipped a beat.

Renata's car still sat in the same spot.

Maria stayed calm as she buckled Layla into the car in the garage. Her hand shook and it took three tries to get the key into the ignition. She started the car before she opened the garage door. The moment the door was up enough for the car to fit, Maria put the car in reverse and backed out.

Renata's car door swung open.

Maria kept backing up. She maneuvered around the woman's car, but Renata ran up to her window.

"Mommy, look..."

"We have to go get the ice cream now, Layla." She knew her voice was on the edge of hysteria. "We don't have time to visit with Renata and Fiona right now, sweetie."

"Maria, you have to stop. I need to talk to you." Renata's voice was muffled through the closed window.

Maria kept backing up. In the rearview mirror, she saw another car pull into her drive. She turned the wheel to go around, but another car pulled in and blocked her way as well.

"Mommy," Layla cried out.

Maria wanted to comfort her daughter but she had no time. Putting her foot on the brake, she shifted into drive. Renata walked towards the car. Maria hit the gas and lurched forward into the yard.

Layla began crying.

Several more cars pulled up to block her escape. Men jumped out of the cars and began running towards their car.

Maria whipped the wheel around so she could get past them but as she did, her car door opened.

"Maria, stop the car now before someone gets hurt," Renata's husband ordered.

"No. Get away from us," Maria screamed.

Layla's crying turned to wailing.

He grabbed Maria's arm through the car window. She pulled away and tried to close the window, but he was quicker and stronger. He grabbed the ignition key and turned the car off.

Desperation set in as she heard the motor die.

"Calm down, Maria. Whatever is wrong, I'm here to help you."

"Liar. Get away from us," she yelled. Maria could hear Layla still crying in the backseat. She jumped out of the car and began flailing at the man.

A neighbor yelled from her front porch. "Maria, are you OK?"

Help. She can get me help.

Maria yelled, "Call 911. Hurry."

Maria watched as Raymond marched across the yard. He hadn't been at the office like he'd told her. He must have been right around the corner waiting for Renata to bring Layla to him.

Falling against the car, she began to sob.

Raymond came up to her. He hissed at her through clenched teeth. "Maria, what are you doing? Do not cause a scene. You're scaring Layla."

Hearing her daughter's name, she pushed Raymond away from her. "You get away from us, Raymond. We're leaving and you can't stop us."

He stepped close to Maria and whispered in a tone so cold her heart froze. "I am taking my daughter, Maria. We can do this the easy way or the hard way. The easy way means you will see your daughter again. The hard way means you will never see her again. It is your choice, Maria. Look around you. You can't stop me." He meant every word.

Maria's only hope was that the police would get here soon. She looked at Renata, who stood behind the men. She turned to the woman.

"Please, don't let them take my baby," she implored Renata.

Maria saw that Renata's eyes glittered bright with tears, but she hung her head. She wouldn't or couldn't help.

Raymond reached into the car and unbuckled Layla. He spent a few moments calming his child and then gave her a kiss. "It's OK, honey. Your mommy is just tired. You go with Aunt Renata, and I will see you in a little bit."

"But Mommy is crying."

"I know. I'm going to take care of Mommy, and then I will come see you." He handed Layla to Renata, who turned and walked away without another word.

"I don't want her to go." Maria sobbed.

"Stop it. You are scaring her. You give her a kiss good-bye and tell her that everything is fine." His tone was firm.

Maria did as she was told.

He nodded at the other men. They turned and walked back to their own cars.

Maria hoped that the neighbor had called the police, but there was no sign of her or the police.

Raymond took hold of Maria's elbow and guided her back to the house.

Maria tore loose from him. "This is insane, Raymond. What are you doing?" she yelled.

He looked at her, his black eyes cold. "It is none of your concern."

"You're nuts. I'm calling the police." She moved to pick up the phone.

"Do what you must. Just remember, I have Layla. What you choose to do will have a great impact on what happens to her."

Maria stopped walking.

He looked at her with such hatred it chilled her very soul.

The ringing of his cell phone broke the spell. He listened for a moment and then hung up. "The police will be here in a moment. If you want Layla to stay alive, you will tell them to go away."

The doorbell rang.

"Go." He pushed her towards the door.

She wiped away the tears. She had to keep Layla safe.

Two police officers stood on her porch with grim expressions. She smiled. "Can I help you?"

The woman officer stepped forward. She was of medium height and stocky, probably in her mid-thirties. Her brown hair was cut as short as a man's. "We've had report of a domestic disturbance here, ma'am. Can we come in and talk with you for a few moments?"

Maria chuckled, hoping to sound casual. "I was afraid that was going to happen. I'm sure some of my neighbors called, but it wasn't really a problem. I could see how someone else might have thought that it was."

The woman officer smiled with understanding. "That's nice, but can we come in and speak with you for a few moments?"

Maria felt her heart palpitate. She had to get rid of these people. If she failed, Layla's life would be in danger. Only moments ago, she would never have believed Raymond would hurt his own child "It's not really necessary. Everything's fine."

The male officer stepped forward. "Ma'am, we're going to have to insist you let us come in. We'll make the determination of whether everything is fine here."

Maria took a step back. "I didn't mean you couldn't come in. I just didn't want you to waste your time."

The officers came into the house. Maria introduced herself and Raymond.

Again, the woman officer took control of the situation. "We received a report of a domestic disturbance. The neighbor said your daughter was dragged out of the car and taken away."

Sweat trickled down Maria's back but she managed a weak smile. "I can see it looked like that. I had to get my daughter to her swim lesson. When our friends pulled in, I was just going to go around them, but one of them offered to take her to swim lessons." She shrugged. "So, I let them."

"Swim lessons, huh?" The male officer didn't believe her for a second.

She nodded and smiled. "That's right. I'm sorry you wasted your time."

"And then what happened to all your *friends*? They just happened to leave?" the man asked.

"You look like you've been crying, ma'am," the woman officer stated.

Maria didn't know what to say.

Raymond stepped to her side. "Officers, my wife tends to be a bit high-strung. She gets overwhelmed at times and this just happens to be one of those days. She forgot to take her medication today."

With those words, Raymond pulled a prescription bottle from his pocket and handed it to the officers. Maria's jaw fell open. She didn't take any sort of prescription medicine. She was about to protest but stopped. She had to keep Layla safe.

"Renata Hannah stopped by for a visit and realized something was wrong with my wife. She panicked and began to call everyone she could think of to help. We all just happened to get here at the same time. You can certainly call her if you wish."

Raymond shrugged while Maria stared at him slack-jawed. Who was this liar?

The officers looked at Maria with pity in their eyes. Raymond was winning them over, not that it mattered. She would say nothing to jeopardize Layla. It took several more minutes and a phone call to Renata Hannah, but eventually the officers were convinced and left.

Maria shut the door and glared at Raymond.

"You did a good job, Maria. I knew you could do it." He looked at her with cold black eyes. "I am not here to argue with you. As I told you, we can do this the easy way or the hard way. The easy way is you cooperate with us, and you get to stay Layla's mother. The hard way is I kill you."

Maria stared in horror at her husband, believing every word. She'd been married to a monster all along, but had been too blind to see it.

"What is your decision, Maria?"

"I'll cooperate." Her voice was low with no emotion.

"Good. I thought you might." His cold dark eyes glittered with hatred as he smiled at her.

****

The phone rang, jarring her from her memories and back to the present predicament.

She stared at the screen. It wasn't Raymond. A Sunberry area code.

She pressed the talk button and said, "Hello."

"Veronica? This is Conrad...Travis...the police officer. Where are you? We have some questions we need to ask you."

Why would they need to ask her questions? Maybe Raymond wasn't lying. Maybe he really had kidnapped Emily.

She took a deep breath. *Be calm.* "I...I had a family emergency. Had to leave town."

"But where are you?"

"Did you find Emily yet?"

"No. And as I said we have some more questions for you."

She closed her eyes. *What a nightmare.* "This is a bad time. There was something I forgot to tell you. I saw a man hanging around the square the past few days. He looked suspicious. Maybe, he took Emily."

"Did he have black hair and a dark complexion?"

A description of Raymond? What was that about? "No. he had brownish-blond hair and a beard. Why?"

"I can't say. I need you to come in and make a sketch of this man you saw."

The tone in his voice said it all. He didn't believe her. But he wanted her back in Sunberry for a reason—maybe Raymond was the reason. Raymond had black hair and a dark complexion. *What if Conrad was working with Raymond?*

"I'm sorry. I have to go." She clicked end once again. The phone rang. Sunberry again. Reluctantly, she hit the answer button. "What?"

"Veronica, what's going on? I know you're in some kind of trouble. Let me help you."

He sounded sincere and she wanted to tell him the truth. All of it, but she couldn't. "I'm fine. Like I said, I have a family emergency. I saw the man leaning against a brown van. I don't know if it belonged to him or not. I hope that helps."

"Veroni—"

"Sorry, I really have to go." She clicked the end button.

The phone rang again. Not Sunberry this time. Raymond. It wouldn't do any good to talk to him again. He might have Emily, but there was no reason for him to hurt her. Emily wasn't a child to him—just a tool to get what he wanted. He wouldn't hurt her until he had what he wanted. Layla

She hit the power button and watched the phone

power down.

    She put her head in her hands and sobbed.

17

After pulling herself together, Maria walked back into the hotel room.

Layla was sitting cross-legged on the bed. She pointed at the TV. "Mommy, we're on TV."

Maria turned towards the TV.

A picture of Maria with blonde hair flashed on the screen along with a picture of Layla. Her most recent school picture. Then another picture flashed of Maria with her natural black hair.

She flopped on the bed, hoping Layla couldn't see how upset she was.

Maria stared at the TV, barely able to breathe. *This was bad—so bad.* People would recognize them and call the number flashing across the screen. She'd never make it to Florida—to Patti and Jamie Jakowksi.

Her plan was crumbling.

The perfect blonde newscaster spoke into the camera, looking both sincere and serious at the same time. "Police will not confirm nor will they deny that they are looking for this woman and child. They were going by the name of Veronica and Jasmine Minor here in Sunberry, Ohio, but those names are believed to be aliases. There is some confusion as to whether the child posing as her daughter is truly her daughter or another kidnap victim. This all came to light with the kidnapping of seven-year-old Emily Most from this small Ohio town."

A picture of Emily Most flashed on the screen.

The fake blonde put a somber look on her face. "It's horrendous when this happens anywhere anytime, but it's particularly devastating to this close-knit community."

"Mommy, why are they saying we know where Emily is?"

"Because they're confused." Her heart was racing and her breathing turned ragged. Not an anxiety attack in front of Layla.

She forced her breathing to slow down. What were they going to do now? It sounded as if a nationwide manhunt had been launched. For her—for them.

That manhunt would lead Raymond right to her.

She reached for the remote and shut it off.

She had to get to Patti as soon as possible.

****

Conrad stared open-mouthed as he watched the news on the wall-mounted TV in the squad room.

Ben Martin bellowed. "How did this happen? What is going on? Where did this woman get this information? It's not even true, as far as I know."

Conrad shook his head. "I have no idea. Maybe the state police gave it to them?"

"Before giving it to us? If that's true, heads are going to roll. I don't care how small of a town this is, there are ways to do things and ways not to." Ben marched to the phone on his desk and hit some numbers. His foot tapped as he waited for someone to answer. "Chief of Police Ben Martin here and I want to know what is going on over there. Why is the TV reporting you have a suspect?"

As he listened, Ben's face turned scarlet. Finally, he screamed into the phone. "I'm coming over there, and you better have some answers for me when I get there."

He clicked the off button and stared at the phone as if he was thinking about throwing it against the wall. "I miss the old phones when you could slam them down. He claims not to know what's going on, either. They claim the information didn't come from them. They're trying to round up the newscaster, but she's nowhere to be found." He stomped towards the door.

Conrad stood. "I'm going with you."

Zink looked up from the computer screen. "Me, too."

Ben shook his head and pointed at Conrad. "You stay here and see what you can find out about this Veronica woman. The search starts at 4 PM at the lake. Meet us there. Keep calling Nick. Tell him to hold down the office here while we search. If he's finished with his nap."

"Fine. I'll keep trying to call Veronica back, but she's not answering. It's going straight to voice mail. She probably shut off the phone."

"Hopefully, the tech guys at the state police will be able to locate her from the phone call. Let me know the minute they do."

18

Maria sat on the bed, and then jumped back up. Panic threatened to overcome her, but she couldn't let it win. Wouldn't let it win. She sat back down. Staying in control of her feelings would keep her alive—and more importantly, Layla.

"Time to go, sweetie." She jumped up and started repacking their escape bags.

"I'm confused."

Join the party. "Me too. We'll talk about it in the car." She'd wanted to ditch the rental, but for now, she'd have to use it. She didn't want to risk going to another rental place and being recognized. For all she knew, her name might be red-flagged, and the minute she tried to rent a car or buy a bus ticket, they'd have her.

Glad she'd paid for the room up front, she hurried Layla out. She took a last glance around the room. Her gaze fell on the cell phone on the bed. She hated the thing. She picked it up anyway.

Once in the car she found the exit for 71 South, the route towards Florida. Patti and Jamie would help her. They would keep Layla safe from the monster. Maria wiped away tears as she drove.

"Mommy?" Layla's tiny voice jerked her back to the present.

"Yes, sweetie?"

"Why are you crying?"

"I'm worried about Emily, sweetie." She couldn't admit she was afraid for Layla as well. Her daughter had experienced enough in her short lifetime. Maria wouldn't add to it.

She drove slow and steady. The last thing she needed was to be stopped by a state patrolman. Time and time again, her attention went to the gas gauge. Sooner or later, they would have to stop.

****

After the chief and Zink left, Conrad stared at the computer for several minutes. This case was like a jigsaw puzzle that had missing pieces.

He picked up his cell phone and scrolled through the names. When he found the one he wanted, he hit enter and waited. "Hey, Leonard. This is Conrad Travis."

"Hi, haven't heard from you in a while."

"I know. Trying to keep busy."

"I don't have anything new for you. You know I'll call you the second I do."

"I know that. But we got all kinds of crazy here right now."

"In Sunberry?"

"A little girl was kidnapped. We're treating it as a stranger abduction. "

"I hadn't heard. What do you need from me?"

"I need you to do some background searches for me, if you don't mind."

"Not a problem, buddy. Give me the names."

"Well...there's a woman here. Her name is Veronica Minor but a few months ago, she was living in Utah under the name of Ramona Dye. She has a daughter named Jasmine. Don't know if the daughter had a previous name. Also a David Hamm from New York."

Conrad tapped his fingers for a moment. "And Nick Johns. There's no rush on the last name. He works for our department part-time, and I'm getting bad vibes about him, but it doesn't have anything to do with the missing girl."

"Got it. I'll get back to you as soon as I can with the first two."

"Thanks."

19

Conrad looked at his watch. Three forty-five and he still hadn't been able to get hold of Nick Johns. Veronica wasn't answering her phone, either. Time to rejoin the search for Emily.

He slugged down yet another cup of coffee, hoping for another caffeine boost. It had been almost twenty-four hours since the little girl had gone missing and longer since he slept.

Their window of opportunity for finding her safe had come and gone. Statistically speaking, it was now just as likely they would find her dead as alive.

He sent up another prayer for Emily.

After a quick call to let the dispatcher know there was no one in the office, he stood. He wouldn't miss the search because Nick Johns needed a nap and had shut off his phone.

At the lake, he parked his car in the parking lot and walked the rest of the way, just like every other volunteer. No special treatment for Sunberry's police department.

A woman in a state police uniform stood on a crate trying to get the volunteers' attention and not having much luck. He watched as Zink inched her way up to the front, and then put two fingers in her mouth.

An ear-splitting whistle brought gazes towards the front.

The woman grinned from her perch on the crate, and then looked at the crowd. "OK, this is the way it works. You will be assigned to an officer, and the two of you will be given a map. That's your area to check. Now when I say check, I mean check. Look under every bush, tree hollow, or hole big enough for a six-year old to hide in. Any questions?"

When nobody asked a question, she nodded. "Go over to the table with your picture ID, sign in, and get busy. And thanks so much for your help."

The crowd made their way to the volunteer table.

The woman hopped off the crate and held out a hand to Zink. "Thanks for the whistle."

"No problem. I'm Suzanne Zinkleman. I work for Sunberry Police."

Conrad walked up.

"And this is Conrad Travis. He's with the department as well."

"I'm Darlene Mays. State Police. I work out of Cincinnati, but they brought me in to help." She put a hand on a hip. "I'm sure you guys aren't happy with us taking over, but…"

Conrad shook her hand. "We appreciate all the help we can get. All we want is to bring Emily home safely to her parents. It doesn't matter to us who does the finding. Any leads?"

She bit her lip and shook her head. "Nothing promising. The little girl seems to have vanished. We double checked the pervs in the area but it's not getting us anywhere."

Zink wiped at her eyes. "Have you spent much time with the parents?"

"Not me personally. Why?"

Zink put shaking hands in her pants pockets.

Conrad knew this was tough for her no matter what she was saying. "No reason. The family are good people, and Emily is such a sweetie. I remember when they adopted Emily."

"Adopted Emily? That's news to me." Darlene Mays sounded surprised.

Conrad had forgotten Emily was adopted, as well. Of course, Zink wouldn't forget something like that. It was a woman thing—probably. Conrad looked over at the growing crowd of searchers, and then back at Darlene Mays. "Does it matter?"

"Everything matters in a case like this. I have to stay here to keep things organized. Do y'all know these woods?"

Zink nodded. "My property adjoins them on the other side."

"Great. Take a few of the volunteers with each of you. Mark will give you a map with the grids for you to cover."

"Not a problem." Conrad gave her an easy smile. "We want to help however we can."

"You are."

In less than two minutes they had their maps and search teams. Zink took two men and he took one.

Sam owned a restaurant in town and was on a first name basis with all the officers.

"Sam, I need a minute. Gotta make a phone call."

"Sure thing."

After the phone call, they moved from tree to tree checking for Emily. At each bush, Conrad or Sam dropped to their knees and went in as far as necessary. Since it was early spring, the leaf growth was minimal so that made searching easier.

Conrad was glad of that. After an hour or so, his

knees had grown weary and his back stiff. "I'm getting old, Sam. This is killing my back."

"I hear you." Sam patted his ample belly. "This doesn't help, either."

"We're almost done with this section." Conrad stretched his back in an effort to relieve the pain.

"Oh no."

Conrad turned towards Sam. "What is it?"

Sam pointed at the shallow creek that ran through the woods. "There's something in there. Looks like a body? See it?"

Conrad walked up beside Sam, his gaze moving in the direction Sam pointed. His stomach twisted. "I'll go look."

Sam's jaw dropped open, and then he nodded. "What do you want me to do? Go get the chief?"

"Not yet." Conrad stepped into the creek. Wetness invaded his shoes. This was the worst possible scenario. He'd prayed for Emily to be safe and sound. The body was face down in the creek. As he leaned down, his cell phone slipped out and tumbled into the water.

After picking up the ruined cell phone, he knelt down and felt for a pulse. The skin was cold to his touch.

Sam stood at the edge of the creek.

Conrad called to him. "My phone's ruined. Can you call Ben Martin?"

Sam pulled out his cell phone and scrolled through a list. Conrad sloshed out of the creek and took the offered phone. He was only wet up to his knees. The creek wasn't that deep.

"What you got, Sam?"

"It's not Sam. It's Travis. I need you over in grid

eight at the creek."

"Did you find Emily?"

20

Conrad's throat closed as he stared at the body still in the creek.

The chief asked again, his voice shaky. "Did you find Emily?"

"Just get over here."

"I'm already on my way. I'll call Zink."

"Conrad shut the phone and handed it back to Sam.

He didn't look very good. He was pale and beads of sweat had popped up on his forehead. "You OK??"

Sam nodded but his eyes never left the body. Finally, he tore his gaze away and looked at Conrad. His voice shook. "I can't believe this."

"You and me both."

"Are you going to call the state police?"

"I wanted the chief here first."

Sam took a deep breath.

Zink jogged up to them, slightly out of breath. "What do you have? Did you find Emily?"

"We found a body." Conrad pointed at the creek. "But it's not Emily."

Zink's eyes widened. "Not Emily. Who is it?"

"The reporter we've been trying to find to get some answers."

Zink's gaze followed his finger. "Guess we aren't going to get those answers now."

Sam still stood there staring at the dead woman.

He turned to Conrad. "Shouldn't we get her out of there?"

Conrad shook his head. "No. The medical examiner will do that. "

The chief, red-faced and out-of-breath, rushed up to them.

Before he could ask, Zink told him. "It's not Emily. It's the blonde reporter. The one who reported Veronica Minor was a suspect in the kidnapping of Emily Most."

The chief's mouth fell open. "You've got to be kidding. Why would anyone want to kill her?"

Zink's gaze met his. "Well if I was Veronica Minor, I might be a tad upset that she put my picture on the TV and told the country I was a suspect in a kidnapping."

Zink had a point, but he couldn't believe Veronica had anything to do with it. When he'd talked with her, it sounded as if she was nowhere near Sunberry. "Or the person who fed her the information and didn't want to be identified."

Zink locked gazes with him. After a moment, she shrugged. "Could be that, too."

The chief shook his head. "Veronica Minor again. That woman's name just keeps popping up in this investigation. Did you ever get hold of her?"

Conrad turned to Ben. "I tried several more times, but it kept going to voice mail. I never got hold of Nick, either. So the station's officially closed at the moment."

"I'd sure be interested in hearing her alibi for this woman's time of death." The chief sighed. His rusty mustache twitched. He reached for his radio. "Guess I better call this in."

****

Conrad wiggled his toes in his damp socks as he sat at his desk watching the pandemonium unfold. His pants were almost dry. It had been insanity since the body of the news reporter was found.

Conrad picked up the phone on his desk and dialed Veronica's number. He knew it by heart now. Hopefully, she would answer this time.

The chief walked over and perched on the side of his desk. "Can you believe this craziness?"

The call went directly to voice mail—again. Conrad hung up his phone as he nodded towards the gaggle of reporters congregating on their sidewalk. "You'd think it was the President of the United States."

Zink pulled up a chair. "What's next, boss?"

"Anybody ever find Nick?" Conrad asked.

"No, but when things calm down, he and I will be having a long talk. And it won't be pretty." Ben Martin stood up. "It's been a long few days. Go home and get some rest. We go back to our regular work rotation as of tomorrow. The State Police and the Sheriff's Department are running the homicide and the kidnapping. The FBI will provide support. They'll keep us in the loop. Who knows what's going to happen next?"

"If anyone wants to call me, you'll have to call my home phone." He fished his ruined phone out of his shirt pocket. "This isn't working any longer."

The chief shook his head. "Will you be at home if I need you?"

"Until the morning. I'm beat." He stood. "So, I guess we stop looking for Emily?"

"I didn't say that, did I? Let's go home."

"I'm going to try Veronica's number one more time."

21

Maria replaced the gas nozzle in the pump, and then slid back into the car. She handed Layla a twenty dollar bill. "Go into the station and get some snacks for us. And not all candy, little missy."

"By myself?" Layla sounded incredulous.

Maria nodded. "And go to the bathroom while you're in there."

"I don't have to go."

"Go anyway. I'll be out here waiting." *And watching.* She prayed no one would recognize Layla from the TV reports, and figured there was a better chance for them to blend in if they weren't seen together.

As she picked up her cell phone and turned it on, her gaze remained on Layla. Maria quickly scanned the missed calls—several from Raymond and several from Conrad Travis.

She didn't want to talk to either man. Her hand shook as she moved to shut off the phone again, but it rang before she hit the power button.

The number said Sunberry Police Department. It must be Conrad again. She sighed and hit the talk button. "Hello."

"Veronica, this is Conrad. Where are you? You've got to tell me what's going on. I know something's wrong. I can help."

Nobody could help. "I can't tell you."

"Are you in trouble?"

"It's nothing for you to worry about."

"Then, why won't you tell me where you are. What's going on?"

Her eyes were glued to the door. She couldn't see Layla. Her pulse raced. "I already told you it's a family emergency." That was certainly the truth.

"Veronica, I want to help you, but I can't if you won't tell me where you are and what's going on." He sounded sincere.

She wanted to believe him, to trust him. His kind eyes and cute smile flashed in her mind. She believed him, but what would be the point in involving him?

She sighed. "Look, I'll be back in a few days. I just have to get Lay...Jasmine somewhere safe, and then I'll come back and help in any way I can." She clicked the phone off before Conrad could speak again.

Her gaze searched for Layla, but no success. It was taking too long. She opened the car door and walked into the gas station. No Layla.

Her mind refused to believe. She moved through the aisles—faster and faster, her heart beat speeding up with each empty aisle. *How had Raymond found them?* At the very back of the store, Layla stood by the soda cooler.

Maria's heartbeat slowed. "What's taking you so long?"

"Oh, Mommy. There's so many kinds. I didn't know what to pick." Her daughter pointed at the top shelf. "And that's the one I wanted, but I couldn't reach it."

Maria opened the cooler door. "I can fix that." She picked up two bottles, one for Layla and one for her.

"Thanks."

"You're welcome. Did you find some tasty snacks?"

Layla held up her goodies. "I got you an apple, Mommy."

"Well, aren't you the best daughter in the world?"

Layla giggled.

They walked to the register. She and Layla put their items on the counter. As the clerk rang up the items, Maria's gaze moved towards the television.

Her heart plummeted.

Her picture filled the screen and a disembodied voice announced that an arrest warrant had been issued. Now a picture of Layla popped up on the screen. Now the two of them were side by side, her Ohio license photo and Layla's school picture.

"Eighteen dollars and forty-seven cents."

Layla reached up over the counter and handed the clerk her twenty dollar bill.

Maria's gaze flitted to the other customers waiting in line behind her. None of them seemed to notice her or Layla. She had to get out of here before they did. She grabbed the sodas and handed them to Layla. Then she picked up the other things. "Come on, sweetie. Let's go. We gotta get moving." She fought the urge to run, but knew that would only bring unwanted attention to them. She opened the door and Layla walked out.

"Hey, wait a minute."

Her heart sank. Someone recognized them. She turned, prepared to do what she had to get out of there and back to the safety of her car. The clerk stood in front of her holding out his hand. "You forgot your change."

"Oh, thanks." She quickly took it and walked to the car, the words from the TV running through her mind. Warrant for her arrest. Suspect in the kidnapping. FBI. What was she supposed to do now? Should she turn herself in?

If she did that right now, what would happen to Layla? Nothing good, that was for sure. Layla alone without anyone watching out for her would make her more vulnerable to Raymond.

Maria wouldn't do that, but she needed to rethink her plan.

Layla was in the back seat and buckled when Maria reached the car. Maria slid into her seat and turned back to the steering wheel. "OK, ready to rock and roll?"

"Mommy, you are so funny, sometimes."

She smiled, glad to see Layla happy for the time being. Turning the radio volume up, she sang along to the oldies.

Layla quieted in the back seat.

A quick glance confirmed what Maria had suspected. Her daughter's eyes were closed and her head lolled against the seat.

Good, she was asleep. It would give Maria time to think about the FBI and the arrest warrant and what she should do. After weighing her options, she made her decision.

22

"David Hamm, with the address you gave me, doesn't exist as far as I can determine."

"Why doesn't that surprise me?" Conrad sat on his couch in his sweats with BowWow half in his lap. He rubbed the golden retriever's head while he talked to Leonard, his FBI contact and friend. "What about Veronica Minor?"

"That's where it gets interesting. Her records are sealed, and I couldn't get access to them."

"But you're the FBI."

"I know that."

BowWow rolled over to allow Conrad better access for a belly rub.

Conrad obliged. "I thought you guys had access to everything everywhere."

"You've got us confused with the CIA and Homeland. They are the super-cops these days. They get all the good toys."

"Toy envy isn't a good thing. You have plenty of your own, anyway. So, what are you thinking?"

"It could mean several different things. She could be an undercover agent of some sort."

He smiled. "Why would there be an undercover agent running a flower shop in little old Sunberry?"

"My thoughts exactly. Another option could be she's under protection for some reason. It was a U.S. Marshal's file."

"You mean Witness Protection?"

"Yep."

Conrad sat up straighter on the couch.

BowWow crowded closer and gave him a slurpy kiss.

Conrad pushed him away. "Can't you get any information about her? She might be in danger. This Hamm guy was at her flower shop and her apartment. We need to get her in custody right now if she's in danger."

"I'll see what I can do. And another thing, I looked into little Emily Most's adoption records like you asked."

Conrad waited. He knew his friend was about to drop a bomb.

"Turns out her bio father was in prison at the time of her adoption. Basically his rights were taken away without any input from him."

"And..."

"And he got out about a year ago. Hired a lawyer to rescind the adoption, but that was shot down about a month ago. The judge refused to hear the case, and it looks as if the Mosts weren't even made aware of what was going on."

"Got a name?"

"I already sent it to your email address along with a pic."

"Thanks, I owe you one."

"Just one?"

After Conrad hung up, he walked over to the laptop sitting on his dining room table along with a week's worth of newspapers and mail. His mother wouldn't be happy if she saw his house. He accessed his email and checked out the pic, name, and address, and then sent it to the chief's and Zink's phones. Clicking his laptop shut, he jumped up. He had things to do.

First on the list was to get a new phone, but that wouldn't happen until the store opened.

After that, it was time to focus on bringing Emily back to her family, and then finding Veronica Minor before this other guy did.

****

Maria had driven through the night and was back in Sunberry. Coming back had been the best option.

The FBI was looking for her, and with her picture all over the TV, she'd never make it to Florida to Patti's. She couldn't risk being arrested in a strange place with Layla. Conrad was here. He'd told her he would help her.

And she believed him. Her instinct said he would keep Layla safe and that was all that mattered.

She'd tried calling Conrad back on his cell phone, but it went directly to voice mail and she wasn't going to leave a message. She couldn't figure out why he wasn't picking up. He'd told her he was there to help. But now he wasn't taking her calls?

Her stomach knotted. *Oh, well. For better or worse, she was here now.*

She prayed nothing had happened to him.

Since she couldn't get hold of him, she had no choice but to go to the police station. Checking the rental car's clock, he was probably at work, anyway. From the times he'd been in The Bouquet, she knew he worked first shift most days.

Maria pulled into the parking lot behind the police

station.

Her mouth dropped open as she looked around. Her eyes widened at the chaos. Several news vans littered the parking lot with satellite dishes atop them. Small groups of people were scattered around the area talking with each other.

What was going on? Had they found Emily? Hope lurched for a brief moment, and then her stomach twisted. If they had, was she alive? *Oh, please God, let Emily be safe and this nightmare be over.*

A woman broke from the pack of reporters, making a beeline towards Maria. With a glance behind her, she motioned for someone else to follow. A man with a camera moved away from the crowd.

They gap between them closed.

Her stomach fluttered, torn between wanting to know what was going on and being terrified of the cameras. But she had to know if Emily was safe. She rolled down the window. "Did they find Emily safe? Is that what's going on?"

The reporter shook her head and jogged the last few steps to Maria. She pushed a small microphone towards Maria. "Who are you? Do you know Emily?" She leaned into the window towards Maria. "Hey, aren't you the woman they're looking...Veronica..." She turned to the cameraman behind her. "Quick get a close up."

Turning her face away, Maria jerked the car into reverse and backed out of the parking lot. The woman and the cameraman chased behind. She put the car into forward and hit the gas.

The car lurched forward.

"Mommy, I thought we were going to talk with the police. We need to tell them about the bad guys so they can find Emily."

That had been the plan, but hearing that woman say her name had made her panic. If she went back now, it would only complicate matters. The reporter would certainly recognize the car and be all over her—and Layla. "We are, honey. Just not here. Look at all the people. It's too crazy."

Her hands shook has she drove. Exhausted from driving all night, it was getting hard to think. She needed to sleep. Maybe they should go to a hotel and sleep. Then she would find Conrad.

Maria found a quiet spot and pulled over once again. Hitting Conrad's number, she waited for him to answer.

He didn't.

Now what? She couldn't go home and she certainly wasn't going back to the police station. It was a madhouse. There was no way she was exposing herself or Layla to those camera crews again. Her head dropped to the steering wheel.

"What are you doing, Mommy?"

"Thinking, sweetheart."

"About what, Mommy?

Maria smiled. "The police station was too crowded. Officer Conrad's not answering his phone so I was trying to decide if we should go take a nap, and then call him later. I'm tired. How about you?"

"Oh, no, Mommy. We gotta tell 'em about the bad guys first."

Yes, they did need to do that.

"We could tell the other policeman—the woman, remember?"

Suzanne Zinkleman—the other officer? The woman had written her address down so Maria could bill her. She wasn't Conrad, but she would have to do. She'd know how to get hold of Conrad or she could help. "Great idea, Layla. Let's go find that nice police woman, Miss Suzanne."

"Thanks, Mommy. I was thinking really hard 'cause I want to find Emily really bad."

Tears sprang to Maria's eyes. Her daughter was so sweet, so compassionate and loving.

Maybe she could catch Suzanne Zinkleman at home before she left for work for the day. Unfortunately, her address was in a box at The Bouquet. Was it safe to go there?

Raymond could possibly be watching the shop, waiting for her. On the other hand, it was more likely he was at their apartment building watching the flower shop's van. At least that's what she would be doing.

He had to know she wasn't going to open up the flower shop with him on the loose, so there would be no reason for him to be there. No, if Raymond was around, it was at their apartment building.

Raymond wanted Layla.

The Bouquet wasn't the target. It would only take a moment to get the address and phone number, and then they could be on their way.

Maria drove to the square and slowly made her way around it. Nothing looked out of the ordinary. There weren't many people around, of course, but it was early and the town was focused on other things.

Emily Most.

Not surprising, considering the disappearance of one of their own.

Maria drove around the square. Nothing unusual as far as she could see. Nobody near the flower shop or watching it. Good, so far. She turned and drove down the next street.

There was no back parking lot for her shop, only an alley that was rarely used. Driving past, the alley was empty. That was good. Nobody was waiting there, either.

Two minutes. That was all the time she needed.

"Layla, I need you to unbuckle yourself, and then hide on the floor."

"Why?"

She rolled her eyes. Why couldn't children just do what they were told? "Because I need to go into The Bouquet to get Miss Suzanne's address and I don't want anyone to see you in the car alone. Can you do that?"

"OK, Mommy."

She drove around the block as Layla unbuckled herself and slid down on the floor. Maria's stomach churned. She didn't want Layla out of her sight for even a moment, but she had to get that address.

She could take her in the store but that would actually take more time. If she went alone, she could run in and out. It should take under two minutes. And Layla was much safer in the car, hidden, than out in the open with her.

What if Raymond was in The Bouquet? He'd be able to break in without a problem. She had an alarm system, but it wouldn't stop Raymond. Nothing would stop Raymond. He promised that and he meant to keep that unholy vow.

"I'm ready, Mommy."

She sighed. Should she take the chance?

Why had she even listened to Layla? She should have taken her to Patti's as she planned. But she had to do the right thing.

Please God, keep Layla safe while I'm in the shop.

She turned down the alley and stopped at the back door. Turning, she found Layla sitting on the floor staring up at her. She whispered, "Ok, I'm getting out and I'm locking the door. You stay hidden until you hear my voice."

"OK."

Maria wiped her sweaty palms on her pants and took a deep breath. She stepped out of the car and locked it immediately. So far, so good. Nothing happened.

She moved to the back door and hit the code into the alarm box. Buzz. She slid the lock in and rushed to the front of the store. If Raymond was in here, then he had her. If he wasn't, she needed to get in, get the address, and get back to Layla.

She kept low and crept behind the counter. Finding the box of receipts, she grabbed it. Running back through the darkened store, her foot caught on an old board. She stumbled, but grasped the box close. Regaining her footing, she stood up.

A knock sounded on the door.

Her heart plummeted.

"Hey," a man's voice called. "Maria."

Maria not Veronica. Half-crawling, half-running, she propelled herself forward. She had to get out. Had to get back to Layla. She ran through the back door, not bothering to lock it. Pressing the unlock button for the car door, she jumped in and relocked the doors.

"Layla?"

"I'm here."

"Stay down, sweetie." Her hands shook as she put the key in the ignition.

A man appeared at the other end of the alley

blocking the way out.

She started the car.

He jogged towards her. Not Raymond, but it must be someone helping him.

Checking the rearview mirror, the other end of the alley was still empty. She put the car in reverse and hit the gas. She moved backwards. No good at backing up, the car weaved one way, and then the other. But it was the only way out.

The man still ran towards her. Towards Layla.

"Mommy?"

"Stay down. Don't move." If the man didn't see Layla, he might think she was somewhere he couldn't get to her.

"Why?" Fear trembled in her daughter's voice.

She weaved her way down the alley backwards, hitting a trash can. The man was catching up. She couldn't let him near her or the car.

End of the alley.

Finally.

She backed up into the street and turned left away from the square. She fishtailed as she hit the gas. The man ran out of the alley and stared at her.

And then, he pointed a gun at the car.

23

Fresh from his shower and dressed, Conrad poured some kibble into BowWow's dish. "Sorry, buddy. No time for a long walk today." He leaned down and rubbed the dog's head. "Maybe later." Conrad had one foot out the door when his house phone rang. He rushed back and grabbed it. "Hello."

"Got some bad news for your pretty flower lady," Zink told him without bothering to say hello.

"She's not my pretty flower lady. What's the bad news?"

"Just talked with Ben. The powers-that-be gave her a second look and have decided she looks good for the murder and maybe the kidnapping, as well. So she's been moved up to a top priority."

"Hold on." He held the phone in one hand as he locked his door with the other. "OK, I'm back. Have they issued a warrant?"

"Not yet—just a BOLO. But the news reports got it wrong. They announced it as a warrant for her arrest, not a BOLO."

His heart sank. Veronica didn't kidnap Emily—he was sure of that. Well, almost sure, but she was in trouble—he was sure of that, as well. "I've got some info of my own on the pretty flower lady and on Emily Most."

"Do tell, partner."

"I'll tell you all about it at the station. But first I

have to get a new phone, thanks to the bath mine took yesterday."

"See you, then."

****

Maria's throat constricted as the man aimed the gun. She stomped on the gas pedal and the car surged forward. Too afraid to look back, she ran a red light, and then two stop signs to get away.

She finally got the courage to look in the rearview mirror. Empty. But not for long. Sunberry was a small town. The man was probably back at his own car, or with Raymond and searching for them right this moment. The town didn't have many places to hide and he'd seen her rental car so he knew what she was driving.

He'd be searching for her.

She needed to hide. Now! Her whole body trembled. *Can't fall apart, now. Gotta keep Layla safe.*

"Can I get up now?" Her daughter whined from the back seat.

"Not yet, Layla."

She'd been nuts to come back to this town—even if the FBI was looking for her. She should have tried to make it to Florida. It was her job to keep her daughter safe. Instead, she'd driven her right back into the jaws of danger.

Now what was she going to do? Go to Suzanne Zinkleman's house or just disappear again? *God, I need some wisdom.* She waited. Nothing happened except more panic.

A tear squeezed out. She brushed it away.

"Mommy? Can I get up now?"

Maria looked into her rearview mirror. No car—nobody followed her. "Sure, honey."

She couldn't protect Layla on her own. It was hard to admit, but she needed help. She reached for the box of receipts. "I need you to do something important, OK?"

"OK, Mommy."

"Look through the receipts until you find Miss Suzanne's name. Can you do that, sweetie? It starts with an S and a U."

"I knew that."

"I'm sure you did because you are such a smart girl." She tossed the receipt box towards the back. It clunked on the seat.

A moment later, Layla called up to her. "I'm looking."

"It should be right near the top."

"I found it. I think. S-U-Z-A-N-N-E." Triumph lit up her daughter's voice.

"That's the one. Now spell out the address for me."

She did.

Maria sighed in relief. She actually knew the road. Sunberry was a small town. She turned left.

The road led her out of town.

Her eyes moved from the road to the rearview mirror constantly. Still no one followed her. They left the city limits. Not more than five minutes out of town, she found the address from looking at the mailboxes.

An old farmhouse with dark blue shutters dominated the yard. Behind it stood a red barn and to the left, a detached garage. It must have been built as an afterthought. It was definitely newer than the farmhouse.

She pulled in the drive.

Layla unbuckled herself and waited for Maria as she gathered up the escape bags. She grabbed her daughter's hand and they walked onto the porch.

The door opened. Suzanne was still in pajamas. Her mouth fell open. "I didn't expect to see you."

Layla dropped her hand and ran to the police officer. "We came back to help you find the bad guys. We think the bad guys might have Emily."

Suzanne gave the girl a gentle smile and squatted down to be eye level with her. "And do you know who the bad guys are, Jasmine?"

Layla shook her head. "I don't, but Mommy does. And my name's not Jasmine. It's Layla."

Suzanne's gaze moved up to Maria. "Really?"

"Really. Mommy said it was all right to tell you. 'Cause you're not one of the bad guys."

"Well, nice to meet you, Layla. You can call me Suzanne. And your mommy is right. I'm not a bad guy. I'm one of the good guys." She looked at Maria. "And your name is?"

"Maria Hammond. And I'm going to tell you the whole story, but it's long." She moved closer to Suzanne. "And we need to get my daughter somewhere safe first."

"You're on a police officer's porch. Isn't that safe enough?"

Maria's gaze flitted around. "Probably not. I need to hide my car."

Suzanne looked from Maria to Layla and back to Maria. She nodded. "Layla, come inside with me. I'll get my keys, and then you can put your car in the garage."

24

Maria took the keys out of the car and left the safety of the garage. Suzanne waited for her on the porch. *No Layla.*

"Where's Layla?" She recognized the panic in her own voice.

Suzanne held up a hand. "She's fine. She's in the house but I need to tell you something. This may not be the safest place for you right now."

Her heart flip-flopped. "What do you mean?"

"The FBI has issued a BOLO for you. And I'm obligated to turn you over to them."

"They're arresting me?"

"A BOLO is a 'be on the lookout' alert. It's not an arrest warrant, but it's serious. I can't ignore it."

"But...I didn't do anything wrong." Maria couldn't believe it. "Conrad said he'd help me. All I want you to do is call him for me." Her knees shook. She stepped backwards and collapsed on a porch swing. "I...I...didn't do it."

"Maybe, maybe not, but I'm still obligated to take you into custody for questioning."

"No...no. I can't do that. I've got to keep Layla safe. If I'm in police custody, who's going to keep her safe? I can't let him get to Layla."

"Let who? What are you talking about?"

"Someone chased us. He'll take Layla again."

"Who?"

"Her father."

"I thought he was dead."

"So did I, but I was wrong."

Suzanne rubbed a hand over her tired eyes. "What a mess. Let's get you inside before anyone sees you." Suzanne led Maria into her home. "Are you hungry? Need something to drink?"

Layla was sitting on the sofa watching TV. "I'm thirsty," Layla told her, and then looked at her mom. "Please."

"Sure thing. Milk or juice?"

"Juice."

"Come with me."

Layla jumped up and followed Suzanne into the kitchen.

Maria trailed the two of them, her mind reeling from Suzanne's news. What was she supposed to do now? Focus on something else. Get grounded back into reality. She looked around, desperate to normalize the situation. Even for a few minutes. "Your house is great."

Suzanne turned towards her with a smile. Her eyes were kind, compassionate. It was almost as if she knew Maria was drowning in panic and needed to calm down. "It is kind of awesome, isn't it? It was built in the 1830s. I've had to do a lot of work so it keeps me busy, but I love it." Suzanne poured some apple juice for Layla. "I've got a place where you can play or take a nap while I talk with your mom. Is that OK with you?"

Layla nodded her agreement.

Suzanne patted Maria's shoulder as she passed, and then led them down the hall to a room. Suzanne's hand shook as she reached for the knob. When the door opened, it revealed a child's room.

The room was brightly colored with a variety of modular wood furniture including bunk beds. In one corner was a child-size desk and in the other two toy boxes, one red and one blue. It was adorable. And neat—too neat.

No child lived here.

Maria's gaze moved to Suzanne. "I didn't know you had..." Maria's voice trailed off as Suzanne shook her head.

Suzanne's posture warned her not to say anymore.

The policewoman turned to Layla. "There are books and crayons and all sorts of things to play with. Have fun."

Layla carried her juice to the wooden desk and set it down. "Oh, this room is so pretty. Whose room is it?"

Maria saw the tears glistening in Suzanne's eyes. "Layla, it's not nice to ask personal questions like that."

Layla's lower lip trembled.

"Don't worry about it." Suzanne stooped down to Layla's height. "For right now, it's your room. Use any of the stuff in it you want. See you in a bit." She turned and walked out of the room.

Maria looked at the woman, wondering about her tears. "Are you all right?"

She nodded, but didn't say anything.

Maria went back into the living room and weaved her way through a maze of plants. She walked to the huge picture window, watching for suspicious cars. The road was empty. She dropped the curtain and turned back to Suzanne.

Suzanne stood at the doorway between the kitchen and the dining room. "OK, I kept my bargain. Layla's safe. Now tell me what's going on?"

"Why won't Conrad answer my calls? Is something wrong? Is he hurt? "

Suzanne shook her head. "He's fine. His phone's not working. He's out getting a new one. No big deal at all."

As relief made its way through her body, she realized just how worried she'd been about him. Even in the midst of her own problems. "When I couldn't get hold of Conrad, I went to The Bouquet to find your address and someone chased me. He had a gun. You need to find him before he finds me—finds Layla."

Suzanne's eyes widened. "Here in Sunberry? Was it your husband?"

Maria stared. How did she know about Raymond? "I didn't know the man with the gun. I never saw him before, but he must be working with or for my husband. That's the only explanation I can come up with."

"I thought you told us your husband was dead. Or was that another one of your lies? You're going to have to be honest with me or I can't help you." The anger in Suzanne's voice was unmistakable.

Maria had to make her understand before the situation got out of control. "I'm trying. Really. But it's complicated and the truth is I'm not sure what's going on myself. I didn't know he was alive. They lied to me. They told me he was dead, but he must not be."

"Who are they? You're not exactly making sense. Maybe you better start from the beginning. Why do you keep changing your name? And why did you come back at all?"

Maria's fingernails dug into the palms of her hands as she fought indecision. Should she tell the truth or try to bluff her way out? She was so tired of hiding and pretending, feeling like a liar. She was done with that. Her gaze met Suzanne's.

No one spoke for a moment as the two women assessed each other.

Maria took a deep breath. "I'll tell you everything that I know, but I don't think I know as much as I need to. I'm telling you this to keep my daughter safe."

"I'll keep her safe."

"When I saw my picture on the TV, I knew you were going in the wrong direction with the investigation. I had to come back. For Emily's sake. You can't be wasting precious time investigating me. I didn't have anything to do with her disappearance."

Suzanne motioned towards the sofa. "Sit down and tell me."

Maria wiped away tears. "I don't know if I should. I don't know who to trust anymore."

Suzanne touched her arm. "You can't go through life not trusting. Believe me. I know it can be hard sometimes, especially after you've been hurt."

"That's an understatement if I ever heard one."

"I know a thing or two about not trusting people, but it's no way to live."

Maria sat down. "I know."

"I've got to make some phone calls."

Maria couldn't breathe. "To the FBI?"

"Not yet, but I've got to call my boss." Suzanne's azure-colored eyes met hers. "I don't have a choice. And besides, I trust the chief with my life—and yours. And let me try Conrad again. Maybe his number is active again." Suzanne pulled her cell phone out of her purse. "Hey, it's me. I need you to come over to my house right away. I can't explain over the phone, but it's important." She pressed end, and then tried Conrad. She gave a thumbs up signal to Maria. "I need you to come over here. I'd rather not say over the phone."

A pause. "OK. See you in a minute." She shut the phone and stood. "I'll go make some coffee and sandwiches. We're gonna need them."

Maria sat on the sofa, praying she'd made the right decision to trust Suzanne and the Sunberry Police Department. Something about Suzanne made Maria feel safe. As if the two women had more of a connection than police officer and citizen. Her instincts said she'd made the right decision. Then again, she'd thought Raymond loved her. Her instincts weren't all that good, apparently.

Stop worrying. God is in control. Maria forced herself back to the present. Her gaze landed on the bouquet Layla had made up. Had it really only been a few days? It seemed like weeks since they walked up to her and told her Emily was missing.

The flowers were sitting on the coffee table in front of her amidst a unique array of candles and tiny angels. Suzanne hadn't come across as the domestic type when she'd met her at The Bouquet, but in fact, her house had a homey feel to it.

And the child's bedroom? What was that about?

Suzanne walked out of the kitchen with a tray. Just as she set it on the coffee table, the doorbell buzzed.

Maria smiled. "I guess you weren't joking when you said you'd see him in a minute."

"Small-town life. Can't use the traffic as an excuse to be late," she said as she walked to the door.

Conrad Travis walked in. He looked at Maria. No change of expression.

Maria smiled at him. Realizing she was wringing her hands, she stilled them. "You must be a good poker player."

"Fair on a good night." He crossed over and sat in a chair opposite from her. "Didn't expect to see you here."

"I didn't expect to be here. I tried calling you after we spoke last night, but obviously you couldn't answer. Suzanne told me about your phone."

He nodded as his gaze probed her. "So, what's going on?"

Suzanne sat down beside her. "Maria was just about to tell me, but we decided we might as well wait until Ben gets here. No reason for her to have to retell the story again and again."

"Ben's not coming. I just talked with him. He's working on something else."

"But I told him it was important."

"What he's doing is important, too." He turned to Maria. "So...now it's Maria? Not Veronica or Ramona? Hmmm. Interesting." He sat back. "Do tell."

Her stomach twisted. "It's complicated."

"Simplify it." His voice was gentle. "I'm on your side, Maria. You don't have to be afraid. We're not the enemy."

Maybe not. But could they protect her from the enemy? Would they?

Suzanne handed her a cup of coffee from the tray.

"As you know, my name is...was...Maria Hammond. My husband was Raymond Hammond." She stopped and waited to see if there would be a reaction to his name.

Conrad's stare was as pointed as a spear. "Why does that name sound familiar?"

"Raymond Hammond was his Americanized name. His real name was Rahmed Hamed."

After a moment, Conrad nodded. "The terrorist from that yacht party last year?"

Maria nodded. "I...we weren't part of that. But to keep us safe, Layla and I are in Witness Protection."

"Thus, the name changes." Suzanne nodded.

"This is all interesting, but what's this have to do with Emily?"

"That's the point. It doesn't have anything to do with Emily's disappearance." She stared at them, not sure if she should continue or not. "But I might know who did it."

Conrad sat forward.

Guilt stabbed at her. "My husband called me the other night."

Conrad's eyes widened. "Your husband? The dead terrorist? The angel your daughter saw?"

She nodded. "I panicked when I heard his voice. The only thing I could think about was to get Layla as far away from him as I could."

Suzanne set her cup on the coffee table. "So, Layla's angel wasn't her imagination. He was at the school watching her. Maybe watching Emily, as well."

Conrad leaned forward. "The news reported he was killed in the shootout with the FBI."

"That's what I was told." Maria's voice was bitter. "I guess they lied to the American people, too."

"Are you sure it was him? On the phone?" Suzanne asked. "Why would they want to protect him? He was...is a terrorist?"

"Maybe it wasn't him, but someone pretending to be him?"

"It sounded like him, but I can't say for sure.

Every time I talk to him, the panic takes over and I can't think. My mind and my body freeze up." Maria's voice cracked. "I'm so afraid of him. He...he..."

Conrad crossed the room and sat down near her. He touched her arm for a moment before moving away. "That is perfectly understandable. We're going to figure this out together. What did he say?" Conrad asked.

"He said if I gave him Layla he'd give Emily back."

"Wow. He admitted he had Emily." Suzanne sat back against her chair. "Do you believe him? Do you really think he has Emily?"

"I believe he wants Layla. As far as he's concerned, Layla belongs to him. And he will do anything to get her back. Do I trust him not to kill Emily in the process of an exchange?" She looked Suzanne in the eye. "Not in the least. He's a heartless monster."

Conrad asked, "When did he first call you?"

"Two nights ago. The day Emily went missing."

"Why didn't you call us then?" Suzanne's voice held a hint of anger. "We might have been able to figure out where he was by now and have Emily home. Safe."

Tears filled Maria's eyes. Suzanne was right and there was nothing she could say that would change that. She'd been weak and made the wrong decision. "I agree. I know I should have. And I'm sorry. Not to make excuses for my bad behavior, but he took Layla from me once, and I know he'll do it again. I only wanted to protect my daughter"

The room grew quiet.

Suzanne ran her fingers through her hair for

several seconds then broke the silence. Her voice shook as she spoke, "That's every mother's job, Maria. No one blames you for wanting to keep your daughter safe. I understand that. I just think it wasn't the right way to keep her safe."

Maria hadn't expected mercy from Suzanne, but was grateful for it. "I can see that now, I guess. Raymond may be an evil man, but he loves his daughter. I suppose as much as he can love anyone. All I wanted to do was get Layla as far away from here as I could. And I wasn't sure I believed it."

"What didn't you believe?" Conrad asked.

"That he really had Emily. It doesn't make sense to me. If he was at Layla's school that day like she said, all he had to do was walk over and take her. She would have gone with him willingly. They could have been in another country by the time I knew she was missing."

"This is true. He wouldn't have had to kidnap Emily at all. You might be right, Maria," Suzanne said. "You think he's lying? You don't think he has Emily?"

"I don't know what to think. I'm so confused." Maria put her head in her hands. Would this nightmare never be over?

"I can't say that I blame you. This is a bizarre situation. At this point, we can't even be sure it's your husband who's calling you or not. You admitted you weren't sure." Conrad looked at Suzanne, and then at Maria. "I know you aren't going to like this, but we've got to tell the FBI about this. They need to know."

Maria stood up. "No. Don't you see? Someone betrayed me. Someone told Raymond where we were. It could have been the FBI or someone monitoring Witness Protection. I don't know, but the more people you tell about this, the more dangerous it becomes. I'm not worried about me, but I'm terrified for Layla and for Emily. The man is a monster."

"We can't just ignore the fact you're standing in my living room while the FBI has a BOLO out for you. What did you think we would do if you came back?" Suzanne asked.

"I had no idea, but I didn't think you'd expose my daughter to that monster again. The man kidnapped her and tried to kill me. Yes, I'm sure he's dangerous." She lifted up her shirt and pointed to the bullet wound on her stomach.

Suzanne gasped.

Maria's gaze locked with Conrad's. She saw compassion, but there was something else. Protective anger burned in them. She looked away, confused by what she saw—and felt. "He shot me three times. He wanted me to die so he could have his daughter."

"If he's really alive, he's not going to hurt you anymore. Or your daughter. We're going to help you, Veronica...Maria. I promise you and Layla will be safe. You have my word." Conrad's voice was filled with compassion. "Don't panic. You're not alone anymore."

Maria stopped pacing and looked at him. Their gazes met. Her anxiety melted away, replaced with a sense of calm. This was a man she could trust. She moved back to the sofa. "Someone betrayed me. Or he couldn't have found me."

"But you can't be sure someone at Witness Protection betrayed you."

"How else did Raymond find us?"

Suzanne spoke up. "Well...I did happen to see your beautiful daughter on TV talking about her missing friend. It was a national newscast. He might have seen it as well."

Maria's hand shook as she picked up her coffee cup. Could that be true? That Raymond had nothing to do with the kidnapping, but was using it to his advantage? She looked up at them and nodded. "You might be right. I suppose it's possible."

"It would explain why he didn't take Layla that afternoon and disappear." Suzanne stood up. A moment later, she came back with her cell phone. She handed it to Maria. "Is that your dead husband?"

25

Maria looked down at the picture on the cell phone screen and shook her head. "That's not Raymond."

Suzanne bit her lip, obviously frustrated. "Are you sure?"

"Of course, I'm sure. We were married for almost eight years." Her gaze moved back to the picture. Her stomach twisted." But he does look like a younger Raymond. He might be a relative. Why? Who is he?"

"Could he be the man who chased you this morning?"

"It's possible. I didn't get a good look at his face. I was trying to keep from crashing as I was backing up. I paid more attention to the gun than his face."

"Maybe Layla got a better look?" Conrad said.

Maria shook her head. "She was hiding on the floor. Why do you have a picture of him? Who is he?"

"He was outside your flower shop yesterday morning." Conrad said.

"Was he doing something illegal? Why were you suspicious of him?"

"No logical reason at first. Call it a gut feeling if you believe in that type of thing." Suzanne spoke up. "But the more we checked on him, the more his story fell apart."

Conrad nodded as he continued. "He was also at your apartment building according to your neighbor.

And he lied about where he lived. Said he lived in Circleville but airplane records have him flying into Columbus from New York the morning after Emily's disappearance. His name is David Hamm."

Maria's stomach plummeted. "That's too similar to my husband's Americanized name to be a coincidence. He must have something to do with Raymond."

"Do you think this man could be your daughter's angel?" Suzanne tapped the cell's screen.

"There's a resemblance to Raymond, but not enough of one to mistake them for each other. I don't think Layla would, either. "

"Not even from across the playground and the street?"

She knew Suzanne wanted her to say yes. To make it seen more plausible, but she had no idea. "I can't be sure, but my answer says she wouldn't have thought this man was her father."

Conrad interrupted the two of them. "Let's go back to the phone calls for a moment. Is it Raymond calling you? What's your thought on that?"

Another impossible question. Her mind said it couldn't be Raymond and yet she'd heard his voice. She wanted to help, but she didn't have any answers— only more questions. "I have no idea. It's too much to process."

Conrad sat beside her and touched her arm. "I know this is hard. I can't even begin to imagine what you're feeling, but we're here to help. You're not alone."

Her eyes filled with tears as she nodded.

"Speaking of pictures." He lifted his cell phone and showed it to her. "Do you know this guy?"

She looked down. Her throat constricted. "That's

the man who was hanging around the square for the past few days. I thought...he was watching me—us."

"Who is he?" Suzanne peeked at the picture.

"He's Emily's biological father." Conrad tilted the phone so Suzanne could get a better look.

"Biological?" Maria looked up at Conrad.

"Emily's adopted. And her biological father tried to get the adoption rescinded last year after he got out of prison. Apparently, he wasn't too happy that the courts took away his parental rights while he was locked up."

Suzanne sat down beside Maria. "He's the one who kidnapped Emily?"

"It's a good chance. The chief's looking into it as we speak."

"With the FBI?" Maria asked.

Conrad nodded. He looked at Maria. "Back to you. When was the last time you talked with Raymond or whoever the man is?"

"Yesterday. I panicked and turned the phone off after I talked with you."

"I think you should turn it back on. When he calls back, get as much information as you can and try to get him to let you talk with Emily."

"I tried to make him let me talk to her. He refused. The more I think about it I don't think he has Emily at all. He wants me to think that so I'll give him Layla." Relief flooded in. Raymond may be alive and after her, but Emily was an innocent child. Maria didn't want that monster anywhere near any child—ever.

Suzanne gave her a soft punch on her shoulder. Her bright blue eyes glistened with a smile as well. "You know what? I'm with you on this. I think he saw her on TV, called you to make you panic, caught the first flight here the next day, and thought he could steal her away."

"Instead, I went into hiding. He doesn't know where I am."

Conrad stood up and walked a few paces away. "OK, ladies. You may be right, but we aren't sure about any of this yet. You've got to play along with him for now and keep asking for proof that he has Emily. We need him to think that you believe him."

"I have a recording device we can attach to the phone, if you don't mind." Suzanne stood up as well. "That way we can listen to it afterwards."

Conrad's eyes widened and he shook his head. "I won't even ask."

She shrugged. "I record all my phone calls and messages. You know, just in case."

Maria wondered what they talking about.

"I'll be right back." Suzanne walked over to a phone and disconnected a small black box.

"I'm going to check on Layla." Maria left the room. She opened the door expecting to see Layla reading a book or watching TV. Instead her daughter slept on the bed, whimpering.

Maria rubbed Layla's back until the cries quieted. Guilt stabbed at her. Little girls were supposed to dream of being princesses, not have nightmares about bad guys chasing them.

Maria brushed away her own tears. No time for a pity party.

Both Suzanne and Conrad were sitting on the sofa when she came back.

Suzanne attached the recorder and showed her the button to hit if it rang.

Maria looked at her missed call log. "He's called a

dozen times. He's going to be so angry."

"He can't hurt you. You're with us. We won't let anything happen to you or to Layla," Conrad promised.

She knew he believed what he said, but Conrad didn't know how evil Raymond was. Only God could protect them. "He promised me that he would never let me have Layla. He's going to win."

"He's not going to win." Suzanne patted her arm. "You have to trust us."

"Even if he can't hurt us," Maria said. "What if he does have Emily?"

Conrad leaned closer. "I don't think he has Emily at all. He's bluffing. I think you're right when you said he was taking advantage of the situation. He probably saw her on the TV and figured out where the two of you lived and caught the first plane here."

She hoped he was right.

"Why wait?" Suzanne asked. "Go ahead and call him back."

"It doesn't have a number. It just says blocked."

"Give it a try and see what happens."

Nothing happened. Then the phone rang.

She jumped.

"Stay calm." Suzanne hit the button on the recorder. "Tell him you have to talk with Emily before you'll even think about meeting with him."

Maria nodded. "Hello."

"How dare you hang up on me and refuse my calls." His voice was icy calm. "I told you to keep the phone on."

"I needed time to think."

"And have you had time to think, Maria? Have you decided whether you want sweet little Emily to live or die?"

She closed her eyes, imagining the sneer on his face. "I want to talk with Emily. I need to know she's OK."

"I wouldn't hurt a child. Unless I have to. If you force me to, then I will. Emily's fate is in your hands."

Tears fell on her cheeks.

Conrad put a calming hand on her back.

"I want to talk with Emily," she told Raymond again.

"No." She heard the fury in that one word sentence. "She's not here with me, but she's somewhere safe. For the moment. But I am losing my patience with you, Maria. The time has come to make a trade. Emily's life for Layla. And since you're back in town, we need to make the trade. Soon."

She closed her eyes, fighting off the wave of nausea. She opened her eyes. "How do I know you even have Emily?"

"Because I said so. I'm not going to argue with you. It's impossible for her to talk with you at the moment. Maybe later."

Conrad made a slashing motion across his throat.

"If you won't let me talk to her then there's nothing to talk about." She pressed the end button. The phone immediately rang.

"Go ahead. Answer it." Conrad told her.

With a trembling finger, she hit the button. "What?"

"I think you are confused. I'm the one setting the rules. I will let you talk with her next time, and then we'll set up a time and place to make the exchange. Where are you?"

"None of your business."

"It is my business. If we're going to set up an exchange we have to be in the same place."

"I'm not telling you."

The connection went silent.

After flipping the phone shut, she looked over at the two police officers. "Maybe it wasn't the bio dad. It sounds as if he really does have her. This is awful."

Conrad looked at her with compassion in his eyes. "We don't know that. Stay calm. Unless I hear Emily's voice on the other end of that phone, I'm not going to believe him. He also knew you were back in town."

"He must have had something to do with that man chasing me."

Suzanne's doorbell rang.

"It's the chief." Conrad got up and opened the door.

A burly man with red hair and a mustache walked into the living room behind Conrad. "What's going on, Travis?"

Suzanne stood, so Maria did, too.

"This is Veronica Minor…Maria Hammond…and she has told us why she has been hiding here in Sunberry."

Shock graced Ben Martin's face, and then he recovered.

"What about Emily?" Suzanne asked. "Did you find her?"

"Not yet, but the FBI is following up on Conrad's lead."

Suzanne stared at the men. "Are you sure they…"

Ben put a hand on her arm. "I am absolutely sure they are doing everything they can to find Emily's biological father. And I'm praying Emily will be right there beside him when they do. We'll know when they know."

She nodded. "Did you talk to the Mosts?"

"I did and they're feeling very hopeful. Much better than the last time you saw them."

Maria watched the interaction between Suzanne and her boss. She was missing something, not that it mattered. Perhaps, the two of them...

The chief turned away from Suzanne and back to Maria. He gave a small smile that didn't reach his eyes. "I'm sorry, but I have to take you into custody."

26

Maria's heart flip-flopped as she struggled to remain calm. "Custody? But I didn't do anything."

Ben Martin's rust-colored mustache twitched. He pressed his lips together. "I'm sorry, but that's not for me to decide. The FBI issued a BOLO for you, and it's my sworn duty to take you in." He took a deep breath. "If it was my decision I'd reconsider...but it's not."

"At least let her tell you her side of the story first." Conrad said. "You really need to hear the whole story first. Believe me on that."

"Doesn't matter. I still have to take her in."

Conrad stepped up beside her. His hand brushed against hers ever so slightly. It was as if he was telling her everything would be OK. He was here and he would keep his promises. "I understand that, but it does matter, Ben. She's in danger, and so is her daughter. She's in Witness Protection. If you take her in, they'll be even more exposed."

"Witness Protection?" Ben's eyes widened. "Wow. I didn't see that coming."

Suzanne said, "Someone's been calling her claiming to be her dead husband and wanting to exchange Emily for her daughter."

Ben Martin looked down at his shoes for a few moments, no doubt processing the new information.

Maria wanted to jump into his thoughts but decided silence was the better tactic with him.

They waited.

He looked up from his shoes. "The Witness Protection Program, you say?"

Conrad nodded. "It's a long story, Ben. That's why we wanted you to listen before you turned her over to the FBI."

"That sounds like a good idea."

Maria sat back down on the sofa.

Conrad moved to sit beside her. He laid his hand over hers.

Turning her own hand into his, she gripped his and drew strength from his touch. She talked.

Ben listened.

When she finished Maria looked at the man who would decide her fate.

Ben Martin fingered his red mustache and stared at her.

Did he believe her? She fought the urge to say something more, something to convince him, but there was nothing more to say.

"It sounds as if you were in Kentucky at the time of the murder. The FBI should be able to verify that with the gas receipt. I believe you, but..." He looked from her to Conrad to Suzanne. "We have no choice. I've got to take her to the FBI, but—"

"No way. It's too dangerous." Conrad's hand tightened around hers.

Ben held up a hand. "Let me finish. First, we need to talk with the U.S. Marshal handling your case and see how she wants us to proceed. You are their problem...I mean their jurisdiction." He gave a tight smiled.

"Makes sense," Suzanne agreed.

"But someone in that organization might have

leaked Maria's new identity and whereabouts to her husband." Conrad said the very thought that she had.

"True, but not likely." Ben shook his head. "More likely, it happened the way Zink said. Someone saw her on TV and recognized her. It wouldn't take long after that to figure out where they were."

Maria knew if Morgan Reed had only listened to her, she wouldn't be in this position now. They would be far away from here and from Raymond. And Layla wouldn't be in danger once again. On the other hand, she wouldn't be sitting here with Conrad, either. And being near him made her feel safer than she had in the year since this nightmare started.

27

Conrad gave Maria's hand a squeeze. He couldn't imagine all she'd lived through in the past year—the betrayal of her husband and the terror of her child being kidnapped. He was in awe and admiration of her bravery and the strength it must have taken to rebuild her life. He would do what he could to keep her and her daughter safe.

"But someone lied about Raymond being dead," Maria said.

"Maybe. Maybe not. Once you listen to the recording, you might decide it's not Raymond at all." Suzanne held up the tape recorder.

"Let's hold up on listening to the tape and call the U.S, Marshal, first," Ben told Zink. He looked at Maria. "Do you have the number?"

"It's in my phone." Maria removed her hand from Conrad's and got her purse. She handed her phone to Ben. "Morgan Reed."

"Don't you want to talk? Explain what's going on."

"You can. She might believe you. Besides, I want to check on Layla." Maria walked down the hall.

Ben put the phone on speaker, and then hit a number.

A woman answered. "Veronica, what's up?"

"This isn't Veronica. I'm Chief Ben Martin from the Sunberry Police Department. We've got a situation here."

A slight pause. "Where's Veronica? I need to talk to her. Now." The woman's voice held a sense of urgency.

The chief jerked his head towards the play room, signaling Conrad to get Maria.

Conrad knocked on the door but got no response. He opened the door and peeked in.

Mother and daughter were curled on the bed together sleeping. A smile tugged at his heart.

Maria had told them it had been almost twenty-four hours since she'd slept. She needed the rest.

He closed the door quietly and walked back to the living room. He whispered to Ben. "She's asleep and I'm not waking her up. She's exhausted. From what I can figure out, she hasn't slept in almost twenty-four hours. Whatever's going to happen, she needs some rest before it does or she won't be any good to anyone, especially Layla."

Ben nodded and explained the situation to the marshal.

Zink's mouth twitched into a smile and her eyes met Conrad's.

"Don't say it, Zink."

She held up her hands. "Me? I wasn't going to say a thing. But you've got to admit the two of you make a good-looking couple."

"I was thinking the same thing."

The chief ended his call with the Marshal and looked at Conrad.

"What does this Morgan Reed want us to do?" Conrad asked.

"She'll arrange a meet with the FBI, Maria, and herself at a neutral place. Somewhere non-public.

Where they can talk in private."

"Like here?" Conrad asked, but Zink was already shaking her head. He knew she was a private person. The last thing she would want would be for more strangers to cross her threshold. He was surprised she'd been so welcoming to Maria and Layla.

Well, not really. Zink couldn't resist a child in trouble. Ever. But he also noticed a growing bond between Maria and Zink. Probably a good thing for both of them.

Ben shook his head. "I don't think that would be a good idea. I was thinking the motel out by the highway. That's what I suggested to her, anyway. She'll call me back to confirm time and location."

"What's the point of the meet?" If someone had betrayed Maria to her ex-husband's people, Conrad didn't want to make it easy for them to find her and finish the job.

"To let the FBI ask their questions, and then move Maria and Layla to a new location with new identities."

Conrad stared at his boss. Maria gone? Before he had a chance to even know her. It hadn't occurred to him that would happen. But of course, that made sense. They'd been on national TV. Time to move on to another new life. Tough choice, but the right choice, he supposed. Their safety was paramount.

"Now what?" Zink asked.

Ben's shoulder's relaxed. "Let her sleep for now. Conrad's right, she's going to have a tough few hours. The more rest she gets the better for her. Besides, the Marshal can't make it for several hours. In the meantime, I'm going to see what's happening with Emily."

28

"I'm not leaving Layla." Maria glared at Conrad and the others as they sat around Suzanne's dining room table. She couldn't keep her daughter safe if they weren't together. Raymond was out there somewhere. He would find them and take her away from Maria forever.

"I know it's difficult, but she'll be safe here. But if you really want to take her with us, I won't stop you. It's up to you." Conrad's voice was calm and rational.

"Do you really want Layla exposed to the questions the FBI wants to ask you?" Suzanne looked at her. "And the answers you have to give them?"

Maria bit her lip. Neither option was good and as much as she hated leaving Layla, she definitely didn't want her to hear the things she had to say about her father. Ever.

"Zink can take care of her, right? She'll be safe here." Conrad smiled at her with assurance. "No one knows the two of you are here except us and the chief. This is probably the safest place for her to be right now."

Maria considered his words. The FBI would eventually let her go. She hadn't kidnapped or killed anyone. And she had to keep Layla out of sight and away from Raymond. Trusting herself to make the right decision was so hard for her anymore.

Her gaze met Conrad's. Trusting Conrad, she

nodded. "She can stay here."

"Don't worry, she'll be fine." Suzanne smiled. "I have an excellent alarm system I'll set. Nobody's going to get through that system."

Conrad touched Maria's shoulder. "And we've got BOLOs out for Raymond, David Hamm, and his rental car. He won't get close to you or the motel. The FBI and the U.S. Marshals will make sure of that."

Maria knew Conrad believed what he was saying. But he didn't know Raymond or what the man was capable of. She nodded, but said nothing.

"Good," Suzanne said. "Sounds like a plan to me. Maria can go in and answer the FBI's questions, and I'll keep Layla here with me."

Conrad walked over to Maria. "If they ask about her, tell them she's visiting a friend. They don't have to know who or where the friend is. Once they're done with their questions, the Marshals can escort you back, you get Layla, and you'll be off to a new life." Conrad stared at her.

She couldn't meet his eyes. The spark between them was real, but now she would never know if it could have turned into more. "I guess that's how it has to be. But..." What could she say? That she didn't want to go? That she wanted to stay here—with Conrad? That he made her feel safe? But that was crazy talk, she barely knew the man. She certainly didn't know him well enough to trust him. "Fine."

Suzanne cleared her throat. "We have a little time before you have to go. Do you want to listen to the recording now?"

"Good idea," Conrad said. "Maybe you'll decide it's not your dead husband back from the grave. According to Morgan Reed, it's not possible that it's

Raymond. He's dead."

Maria prayed that would be the case—but she didn't have much hope. She knew in her heart Raymond was alive, because she'd never felt safe since the day she'd discovered her husband was a monster.

Suzanne hit the button on the recorder, but her doorbell buzzed at the same time.

"I'll get it." Suzanne walked towards the door.

"How're you holding up?" Conrad leaned close and picked up her hand.

"Truthfully, I'm numb. My mind doesn't seem to be functioning."

"You are a strong woman, Maria. Look at all you've been through, and you're not only still here, but you're smiling most of the time. I have nothing but admiration for how well you've handled all this."

Tears welled up and she wiped them away. "Thanks. That means a lot." She squeezed his hand.

"The chief's back." Suzanne came in, followed by the chief.

Chief Martin sat down and pressed the button on the recorder.

The group listened to the recording two times without comment.

Finally, Ben looked at Maria. "So, do you still think it's your dead husband talking?"

If it wasn't Raymond, then who was it? The thought that it wasn't Raymond terrified her almost as much as if it was. "I'm not sure. It sounds like him, but not exactly. This man's voice isn't quite as deep as Raymond's, but it is still, cold and unfeeling." Hearing the voice made her sick to her stomach. "I can't be sure."

"Maybe Layla could—"

"No way, Ben." Conrad said. "Don't be ridiculous. She's just a little girl who thinks her dad is an angel. She doesn't need to hear him talking about kidnapping her best friend."

The protectiveness in his voice warmed Maria's heart. She looked at him with gratitude.

He smiled back at her.

"Fine, fine. You're right. I wasn't thinking about it from that point of view."

"You certainly weren't thinking, chief." Suzanne glared at her boss. "Sometimes, I wonder about you."

Maria ran her fingers through her hair. "None of this makes any sense. Whether this man is Raymond or not, he has to know I would never let him have Layla willingly. So why would he try to arrange an exchange? He knows it would be a setup."

"Good point, Maria." Conrad's hand rested on her shoulder. "Why is he going through with this charade, whether he has Emily or not?"

She fought the urge to grasp Conrad's hand. His touch seemed to keep her anchored, keep her from crumbling. Conrad thought she was a strong woman, but she had no strength left. Saying a silent prayer, she asked for wisdom and peace.

Chief Martin heaved a sigh as he plopped down in a chair. "Because he doesn't know where you are. He can't take Layla until he can find the two of you."

"Perfect poker play," Conrad spoke up. "So he's trying to force your hand."

Maria nodded. "So, he can steal her away from me again. So, you don't think it was Raymond Layla saw at school?"

"If it had been him at school that afternoon," the chief said, "he would have taken her and been gone before you knew anything was amiss."

"It had to have been her imagination." Conrad paced around the room. "I've heard of this phenomenon before. People believe they see the ghost of a deceased loved one. It's not all that uncommon."

Had that happened to him after the death of his wife?

"Add in the fact, Layla is a highly imaginative young girl and it all makes sense," Conrad said. "It was simply a coincidence that it happened on the same day as Emily's abduction."

"I don't buy it," Suzanne chimed in. "It's too coincidental that she saw him the same day Emily went missing."

"But if it was Raymond, why wouldn't he have just taken Layla and disappeared?" Maria asked. "And how did he find us here?"

Conrad picked up his coffee, but didn't drink. "For what it's worth, I agree with the chief. Maria, you didn't get a call until after Layla was on TV. I think someone recognized her and decided to take advantage of the situation to get her."

"Assuming it's not Raymond," Suzanne said, "who would do that?"

"I can't think of anyone except Raymond or his family," Maria murmured.

Ben leaned forward. "Can you get us a list of his family members?"

"I can't. I thought he was Raymond Hammond from Brooklyn. I don't know a thing about the real Rahmed Hamed." To her horror, tears leaked from her eyes. "I'm sorry. I'm...I'm terrified. I can't think straight. If something happens to Layla..."

Conrad sat beside her and picked up her hand

with a gentle touch. "We understand. We're not going to let anyone hurt Layla or take her from you." The warmth in his gaze made her feel safe—safer than she'd felt in a long time.

She nodded. "There might be someone else who can help."

"Who?" Ben and Conrad asked at the same time.

"His name is Marcus Hanks. He works for the FBI, but I don't know how to contact him."

"That's OK. I do. I have a friend in the FBI. He'll be able to get me some contact information."

The doorbell rang.

"Who is that?" Maria jumped up, panicked.

"It's Nick Johns." Conrad looked out the window, and then turned to Maria. "Another police officer from Sunberry."

"Yeah." Suzanne rolled her eyes. "And one who's been missing for a day. He has some explaining to do as well."

"He's only part-time and he wasn't scheduled to work." The chief said.

"Still, I can't believe he just left and went home and took a nap while Emily was missing. It's pitiful." Suzanne's voice rose with outrage.

"Not everyone has your work ethic." Conrad pointed out.

The doorbell rang again.

Conrad's gaze moved to Maria. "The more people who know about you and Layla, the more likely it's going to become public knowledge."

To have people worried about her—taking care of her felt good. She stood.

"Zink, can you put her somewhere for a few moments until we get rid of Nick?" the chief asked.

"Go back to Layla's room." Suzanne waited for Maria to leave.

Maria hurried down the hall and slipped into Layla's room.

"Hold on," Susanne called. "I'm coming."

29

Not wanting Nick to notice the number of coffee cups, Conrad gathered them from the table and walked into the kitchen.

Zink opened the door. "Well, Nick, nice of you to join us. Did you have a nice nap?" She motioned for him to step in.

Conrad walked back into the living room as Nick entered the house.

"What's that supposed to mean?"

Zink put her hands on her hips. "It means we've been calling you for two days and you haven't bothered to return any of my calls."

"Been busy," he mumbled.

"Nick, I know you're only part time, but I do expect you to be available in emergencies," the chief said. "And this town is in an emergency. It's not like you didn't know that."

Red crept up Nick's neck. "I know that. And normally I would be, but I had my own emergency. My dad had a heart attack."

"Is he all right?" Zink's expression made it clear she didn't believe him.

Conrad couldn't blame her. Trust was difficult for her, too. Probably as much as for Maria.

"He's still in intensive care, but the doctors say he'll be fine. I went to the station and couldn't find any of you, so I went to your house, chief, and then

Conrad's. Finally came out here. I know I have a shift tonight, but I can't work it. I came back to get a few things, pick up my dog, and get back to Cleveland."

Suspicion nibbled at Conrad. He wondered what Leonard might find when he looked into Nick Johns's life. He'd certainly found details about Emily Most that weren't common knowledge.

Conrad excused himself and walked towards the bedroom. The door opened before he could knock.

Maria put a finger to her lips as he slipped in.

Layla was still asleep on the bed.

"She's exhausted," Maria whispered as she caressed her daughter's hair.

A lump formed in his throat. His voice was quiet as he spoke. "So I see. You must be tired, too."

"I slept for a while. I'm feeling much more rested. I just want this to be over."

"Is there anything I can do for you?" he asked. "Really, I want to help."

She stared at him with her chocolate brown eyes.

His heart jumped into his throat. Those were eyes he could stare into forever.

She smiled and touched his cheek. "I'm fine. Really. You being here has been such a...such a blessing to me."

Conrad managed a chuckle. "A blessing? Nobody's called me that before."

She smiled at him. "I have a feeling that's not true in the least. You go out of your way to help others."

"I'm sorry to see you leaving Sunberry. I'd hoped..." His gaze caught hers. "I'd hoped we'd have time to get to know each other."

"Me, too." She looked away. "I'm so tired of all of this. Of running. Of lying. Of being afraid."

He moved closer and put his arms around her. Perfect fit.

She laid her head on his shoulder. "I felt horrible lying to you about my name and everything."

He felt rather than heard her sobs. He caressed her hair while she cried.

After a time, she moved away. She looked up with red, watery eyes. "Thanks, I needed that."

"Glad to be of service. You're going to get through this, Maria. You're stronger than you know. I think you're incredible."

"I'm glad I met you. I only wish I'd gotten to go to that Bucks game with you. Even if you didn't actually invite me to it...yet."

"But I was going to."

She laughed.

****

Conrad cracked the bedroom door in time to hear Zink and the chief telling Nick goodbye. He waited until the front door closed. He motioned to Maria and held the door for her. They went down the hall, close, but not touching.

The chief and Zink were whispering in the kitchen.

Maria went out the living room and sank onto the sofa.

Conrad sat beside her.

"It must be horrible for the Mosts right now," Maria said, uncomfortable with the sudden silence. "I hope they find Emily soon."

"Me, too," Conrad said. "I've seen what it does first hand."

"What do you mean?"

"Oh…um…it's not my story to tell."

"Whose story is it?"

The chief and Zink came into the room. Both looked grim. Conrad nodded his head towards Zink, but said nothing.

"I'm sorry, Maria." The chief's voice was gentle. "But it's time to go. I have to take you to the FBI."

"Don't worry about Layla." Zink reassured Maria. "She'll be right here safe the whole time. Better go say good-bye before you leave."

Maria hugged Zink. "I'm sure she will be. It makes me feel a lot better knowing she's here with you."

****

Layla was sitting up in the bed, her hands clasped in prayer. Her eyes popped open as Maria walked into the room. "Hi, Mommy. I was praying for Emily."

"You're a good girl. Prayer is always the best thing we can do in any situation." Maria held up a plate. "Are you hungry?"

Layla nodded and scooted off the bed. The coloring book and crayons adorned the desk, and toys were scattered on the floor. "Why can't I come out there?"

"Oh, we're talking about adult things. Things you wouldn't even care to hear about."

"If it's about Emily, I do want to hear it."

"I know you do, baby. But remember what I told you about a mommy protecting her child. That's all I'm doing. I won't hide anything from you about Emily. I promise, even if it's bad. But there's no reason to worry about things until we know for sure."

Layla searched her mother's eyes and nodded with apparent satisfaction. "What did you bring?" she asked.

"Your favorite—peanut butter and jelly for two."

"Thanks, Mommy."

"You're welcome, sweetie." After a few bites, Maria continued. "Layla, I have to leave for a while."

"Without me?"

Maria nodded.

"Are you going to find Emily?"

"That would be wonderful if that happened. I can't make a promise, but we're going to do our best."

Layla's gaze was serious.

"Miss Suzanne is going to stay here with you. You'll be safe."

"I want to go with you, Mommy."

"I know, and I want you with me, but you can't. I have some adult things I have to do. You'll have a lot more fun here with Miss Suzanne. Don't worry. OK?"

"OK."

Maria pulled her close. Her daughter had trust in her words as only an innocent child could have. No wonder Jesus had said one must become like a child to enter the Kingdom.

Help me, Jesus. To have that same childlike faith.

"I love you, Layla. You are the best daughter ever."

"You're the best Mommy ever, too." Layla grinned. "I love you, too, Mommy."

"I know that, sweetie." Maria pulled up from the kneeling position. "Layla, if something...oh never mind. I'm not sure when I'll be back. You listen to Miss Suzanne while I'm gone, OK?"

"OK." Layla grabbed her hand and they walked

out of the room together.

She had so much she wanted to say to Layla—in case she didn't come back.

She sucked in a breath. God would take care of her. She'd have a chance to tell Layla everything later.

Maria unclasped her hand from Layla's. Her hand shook as she picked up her purse.

I can do this. I can do all things through Christ who is my rock.

After one last hug, she didn't turn back until she was at the car with Conrad and the chief.

"I'll follow you in my vehicle." Chief Martin went to his own car.

Suzanne waved from the door.

Layla peeked out and waved.

Maria's eyes filled with tears. Would they ever be able to have a normal life? Or had Raymond stolen that from them forever? She answered her own question, knowing God promised beauty for ashes. Somewhere out of the ashes, a better life waited for her and for Layla.

"Ready to go?" Conrad asked as she buckled her belt.

She nodded.

He put the car in reverse and backed out.

She was terrified. But Conrad was with her. He'd promised to keep her safe.

And she believed him.

30

Conrad's gaze swept from side to side, and then back to the rearview mirror. Someone was out there watching for Maria and he was determined to keep her safe.

Her dark, sultry eyes touched him. It was hard to imagine all she'd been through the past year. And yet she was still sweet, kind, and funny.

Her smile made him believe love was possible for him once again. A sad longing filled him that it wouldn't be with Maria. She would have to disappear as soon as the FBI released her. Still, she'd awakened emotions that had been dormant since his wife's death. Love and a full life were possible again. God might still have a few surprises for him.

"So once we get to the hotel the FBI will question you, and when they're done the U.S. Marshals will escort you back to Zink's to pick up Layla."

"I'm so tired of moving."

A spark of hope ignited, but he immediately extinguished it. "I'm sure you are, but they can keep you safe. That's the important thing."

"I suppose you're right."

"But I want you to know that no matter where you end up, if you need me, all you have to do is call and I'll come running."

"Aren't those the words to a song?"

"Close enough." He chuckled. "In fact, go ahead

and put my cell phone number into your phone. Right now. That way you'll always have a way to get hold of me."

"They won't let me keep in touch. It's too easy these days to do an electronic trace."

"Memorize my number and call from a pay phone, then."

She nodded, but remained silent.

They arrived at the hotel without incident. He drove to the back entrance. A man and a woman stood by the door.

"That's Morgan Reed, my liaison with the Marshals."

"I'll drop you off, and then park. See you in a minute." He reached over and squeezed her hand.

Maria rewarded him with a smile and stepped out of the car.

31

Maria stood there as Conrad drove off to park the car.

Morgan hurried to her side. With gun drawn, she escorted Maria into the hotel.

Two FBI agents stood on either side of the door.

Maria was hustled into the room where two more blue-jacketed men stood. Her throat constricted. They didn't look very friendly. Convincing them of her innocence might be harder than she thought.

Her stomach clenched. She was getting a funny feeling. One she didn't like.

"Where's Layla?" Morgan asked. "You were supposed to bring her with you."

"She's at a friend's."

The woman actually gritted her teeth as she spoke. "That wasn't the way it was supposed to happen. Where is she?"

"Why do you need to know?" Maria's instincts were screaming and it took everything she had not to panic.

"Because she needs to be moved to a new location."

She? Not they? Maria's pulse sped up. "Don't you mean *we* need to be moved to a new location?"

Morgan wouldn't look at her.

Maria touched Morgan's arm. "What's the problem? What's going on? I want to know. I have a right to know."

One of the agents stepped forward. He was large and imposing. "I'm Nat Daniels, special-agent-in-charge."

Maria nodded.

Nat Daniels turned to Morgan. "We don't have time for this, Reed. We've got a job to do. You said the girl would be with her. She's not and that's not our problem. You can deal with that later."

Maria backed away. Something bad was happening here and she needed to leave. Needed to get to Conrad.

A second man stepped forward. "Maria Hammond, you're under arrest for the murder of Julianna Vance. Put your hands behind your back." He put a hand on her arm.

"Who is Julianna Vance?" She jerked away from him. "I didn't kill any—"

Two of the other FBI agents forced her to the floor. They twisted her arms behind her back.

"Do not resist arrest." Someone's voice droned in her ear.

Her face was smashed against the carpet and she couldn't breathe. Cold metal cuffs were snapped around her wrists. She was pulled up from the floor by her arms.

She stared at them. This couldn't be happening. She'd thought they were on her side. They were supposed to listen to her, not arrest her. They were supposed to be concerned about Raymond or whoever was calling her. How could they believe she killed someone?

Someone knocked on the door. The agents looked at each other, and then at Morgan Reed. She shrugged.

"Conrad Travis. Sunberry Police Department."

"Who invited him to the party?" Nat Daniels glared at the door and then at Morgan.

"Not me," Morgan said. "I thought he was dropping her off. That was the plan."

Conrad knocked again, louder and more forceful.

Nat Daniels grimaced. "You apparently didn't have your plans straight. We can't have him drawing attention to himself or us. Let him in."

Maria struggled to keep tears from falling.

Conrad must have known what they were going to do, and he hadn't even warned her what was about to happen. Maybe she'd been wrong about him.

The fourth agent opened the door.

Conrad's gaze took in the room full of agents, and then found her. His eyes widened. "What is going on here?"

Morgan Reed stepped in between them. "We all need to stay calm. She's under arrest."

Conrad went to Maria. "Why? You surely didn't have time to listen to her account. What happened?"

She turned so he could see the handcuffs. Her voice shook as she spoke. "They arrested me. For murder." Tears seeped out.

His hand moved towards her cheek. He wiped away her tears. She was grateful for the physical contact. "I'm sorry. I didn't know. Don't worry. We'll work it out." He turned back to the group who stood silently watching them. "We were told you wanted to question her. Nothing was said about an arrest."

Maria's muscles relaxed. Conrad hadn't abandoned her to the FBI wolves.

The leader stepped forward. "It wasn't your business. It was on a need to know basis."

"This woman and her child are my business, and I'm not going to let you arrest her. Putting her in jail will only make her a bigger target." He turned to Morgan Reed. "How could you let this happen?"

"I...I..."

"Don't bother with an explanation. Save it for your bosses." His tone was more than disgusted—it was on the verge of angry.

He hadn't betrayed her.

"Take the cuffs off her. She isn't a danger to anyone."

"She resisted arrest." Nat Daniels told Conrad.

Conrad looked at her. A smile tugged at his mouth and he winked. "Did you resist arrest, Ms. Hammond?"

"Not really. I was just surprised. I reacted without thinking."

He put a hand on her arm and turned to the others. "I don't know why you arrested her, but you're making a mistake."

"No mistake." Morgan said. "Forensic evidence doesn't lie."

"In this case, it does." Conrad's voice was firm. "We have proof she wasn't even in the state at the time of the murder."

Nat Daniels looked at Morgan. "Why wasn't I told about that?"

Morgan's cheeks flamed red. "I didn't know."

"There seems to be a lot of things you don't know, Marshal Reed." Nat looked back at Conrad. "What's the proof?"

"We have her, her car, and her child on video at a gas station in Kentucky at the approximate time of the murder. Along with a receipt with the time stamped on it. There's no way she could have killed Julianna Vance. The time of death is while she was on the road in Kentucky."

Nat Daniel's face flushed red. "Where's the proof?"

"Back at the station. The plan was supposed to be you interviewing Maria, and then we could go back to the station and give you the evidence."

The two men locked eyes as if assessing the integrity of the other. Nat Daniels held out a hand. "I'm Nat Daniels."

Conrad shook the offered hand. "Conrad Travis, Sunberry Police Department."

"I've got your word that this evidence exists?"

"Absolutely."

The two men stared at each other.

Nat Daniels nodded. "Take the cuffs off her."

32

Maria collapsed on the bed as she watched the FBI agents file out of the motel room.

Nat Daniels agreed to go to the station and view the video and the receipt, but as far as he was concerned, Maria was free to go. 'No longer a suspect' were his words to Conrad. As long as the evidence verified what Maria and Conrad had told him.

Conrad and Nat Daniels seemed to have bonded. The two men discussed the case and the evidence. Nat Daniels had even apologized to Maria before leaving.

As the door shut, Morgan Reed turned to her. "I'm so—"

"Don't bother. You need to leave. I am so done with you." Maria was finished with this woman's incompetence.

"I was only—"

"Only what? I thought your job was protecting Layla and me. And you certainly didn't do that. In fact, you haven't been doing it all along." Maria jumped off the bed and marched towards the door. "You need to leave. Now."

Conrad walked over to Maria's side and opened the door. "You heard the woman."

"It's my job to protect her."

"I'll take over that detail. You can have your boss call me at the Sunberry Police Department. I have a few things I need to tell him."

Morgan's face flushed red. Her gaze went around the room. "I can't just leave. Maria, you have to come with me. We'll pick up Layla and—I..."

Conrad opened the hotel door. "You don't have a choice, Marshal Reed."

"Maria, you're making a mistake." Morgan stalked out of the room.

Conrad closed the door. "I'm sorry I brought you here," Conrad said to Maria. "I didn't know they were going to do that."

"It wasn't your fault."

Conrad's phone rang. He grinned as he fished it out of his shirt pocket. "Wow. That was quick. Want to take bets on who it is? FBI or U.S. Marshals? Hello." A smile spread across his face as he listened. "Thanks, chief. That is wonderful news."

"What's wonderful?"

Conrad smiled, lifted her up in an embrace, and whirled her around. "They did it. Emily's safe."

She hugged him back as her feet touched the floor. His arms continued to embrace her. Maria followed his lead and the two danced around the room laughing. After another twirl, she planted her feet and the two bumped to a stop. "Details, please."

Conrad kept his arms around her as he spoke. "According to Ben, her biological father's in custody. She's fine except for being scared, of course. He was arrested without incident trying to cross the Canadian border. She's on her way home now with a police escort as we speak."

"Layla will be so happy"

"Layla happy? I'm the happy one. A beautiful woman in my arms dancing with me." They danced once again.

Maria giggled.

The dance ended and in the next moment, Conrad bent down and their lips touched. Warm and sweet.

Not moving, Maria savored the moment.

Conrad straightened up. "I'm sorry, Maria I shouldn't have done—"

"Oh, yes you should have." She touched his cheek. It will be my very best memory of my time in Sunberry."

Conrad met her gaze. "Then maybe I should give you one more memory?"

She moved closer. "That seems like a very good idea." When they parted, Maria turned away and wiped away tears.

"Maria?"

"I'm fine, really. That is wonderful news. Emily's safe and just like we suspected, Raymond didn't have her. It was all a ruse. Layla will be so happy. I can't wait to tell her." Her phone rang. She looked down at the screen. "It's not him. At least it's not the same number as before."

Conrad walked over. "That's Suzanne's number. Better pick up."

She flipped the phone open. "Hello."

"Mommy." Her daughter's voice was barely above a whisper. "Mommy, the bad man's after me."

33

"What do you mean, Layla?" Maria's heart turned to ice.

"What's happening?" Conrad nudged her, but she ignored him.

"It's the bad man, Mommy. He's chasing me." Terror and panic seeped through the whispered voice.

"Where's Miss Suzanne?" Maria's own voice edged on panic.

"She told me to hide, but he's after me. I had to leave." Her daughter whimpered.

"I'm on my way, baby. Where are you?"

"I don't know." More sobs. "I don't kn—"

The phone went dead.

"What's going on?" Conrad tugged her arm.

She whirled around.

"What's happening? Tell me."

Gulping back the panic, Maria tried to form a thought. "She said the bad man's after her."

"Where is she?"

"She didn't know."

"Where's Suzanne?"

"I don't know. I don't understand." Hysteria overtook her. She clutched her head, taking huge gulps as she tried to contain her terror.

"Calm down, Maria. Tell me what's happening?"

"She told me the bad man's chasing her," she said between sobs.

"We need to get to Suzanne's. Now." Conrad grabbed her hand, and they ran down the hall.

"It has to be Raymond. He found her. I knew he would. I knew he would," Maria struggled to breathe as terror pushed the oxygen from her lungs.

"That can't be true. She wouldn't have called her father a bad guy and she wouldn't have been afraid of him."

A spark of hope. Conrad was right. Layla would never call her father a bad guy.

They arrived at the car. He leaned over and gave her a sweet kiss on the cheek as they slid into the seats. "Come on, Maria, you can do this. Don't panic now. Layla needs you."

Maria called Suzanne's phone over and over. It went directly to voice mail.

While he drove, Conrad called the chief to explain the situation.

As he pulled into Suzanne's drive, she unbuckled her seatbelt. Before the car stopped, she flung the door open and ran towards the house.

Ben pulled in right after them.

Hands grabbed her by the shoulders. The chief's voice penetrated her panic. "Stop. You can't run in there like that. We don't know what's happening. It could be dangerous. I'll go in. You wait out here."

"My daughter's in there."

Conrad touched her chin and guided her face to his. "Look at me, Maria. Don't argue. Let us do our job."

She nodded, not wanting to waste time.

Conrad would do everything he could. They pushed past her and went towards the house.

Her heart raced, and she wiped away the tears. *All*

her fault. She knew better than to leave Layla. Raymond had found a way to reach her.

34

Maria's eyes closed in a wordless prayer. It seemed like a year since Ben and Conrad had gone into the house. What was happening in there?

"Maria."

She opened her eyes.

Conrad stood there; his face mirrored the concern she felt. His hand touched her arm. "We found Suzanne, but not Layla. She's gone."

"Is Suzanne...is...is she dead?"

"No. Just unconscious. The ambulance is on the way. You can come in."

"I don't understand. Where's Layla?"

"We can't find her."

She rushed past him and into the house. Chairs were knocked over, knick-knacks were broken. Suzanne's cozy home was trashed. Several of the plants at the window had been tipped over and dirt decorated the floor.

Ben Martin knelt down beside a very still Suzanne. Her face was pale and she didn't appear to be breathing.

Maria stopped. "Are you sure she's...she's alive?" Dread filled Maria, horror that someone else might die in Raymond's mad scheme. Suzanne had taken her in, listened to her when no one else did.

"She is, but her breathing is shallow. I've called for reinforcements. You stay here with her. We're going to search the house again."

"Are you sure Layla's not here?"

"We searched every inch and called her name. No response."

"Maybe, she's hiding. I've drummed that in her head the past year. If someone chases her, she knows to hide. If she hears my voice, she'll come out."

Suzanne moaned. Her hand reached out for the chief's. "Layla. Gotta get to Layla."

"She's not here." Maria knelt down and touched Suzanne's hand. "What happened? Where is she?"

Suzanne murmured and opened her eyes. She attempted to sit up, but her eyes fluttered shut and her body relaxed. Unconscious again.

"I'm going to go look for Layla." Maria walked down the hall calling. "Layla. Layla. It's Mommy. It's safe to come out now." Her gaze strayed to the window. It was getting dark. Soon it would be night. Tears streamed down her face. She turned and bumped into Conrad.

"It's OK, Maria. We're going to find her." His arms encircled her. "I promise."

"How? He probably already has her. They'll be out of the country before nightfall."

"It's not Raymond. He's dead."

"I know everyone keeps saying that, but he's not. I heard his voice. It's him. I'm sure of it."

"You weren't sure when you listened earlier. That's the fear taking over. Don't let your mind trick you."

"I just didn't want to believe it. My mind was playing tricks then—not now. It was Raymond, and he's alive." She sobbed. "And he has Layla."

His arms tightened around her. "I don't believe

that. She called you. Remember? He didn't have her then. She said she was running away from the bad man. She wouldn't call her father the bad man."

"You're right. I have to keep remembering that. But if it wasn't him, who was it?"

She stepped out of his embrace and swiped at the tears on her cheeks. "Since...since she was kidnapped, I've been teaching her what to do. I hated scaring her, but I taught her to hide and not let them find her."

"There you have it. She must have found a good hiding space. All we need to do now is find it. Like a bizarre game of hide and seek."

Maria took a deep breath, and calmed her aching heart. She had to be strong for Layla. She looked up at Conrad and found a strong resolve to not panic anymore.

"Let's go find my daughter."

35

"I'm OK." Suzanne pushed the medics away as she tore off the oxygen mask. She sat up. "Oh, no. Where's Layla? Did you find her?"

Maria shook her head. She couldn't make herself say the words.

Suzanne rubbed her forehead. "Let me think a minute. Everything's groggy and confused. I can't remember what happened."

"This woman needs to go to the hospital." The EMT glared at them.

"Layla called me and said the bad guy was chasing her. Then the line went dead."

Suzanne attempted to stand up.

The chief put a hand on her shoulder. "Stay on the floor. Give yourself a minute."

Instead, Suzanne used his arm as an anchor. She swayed.

Chief Martin put a protective arm around her back.

"No. We don't have a minute." Her voice shook and her body trembled. "This is all my fault. It was my job. I'm so sorry, Maria. I promised to keep her safe. And I didn't."

"Zink, don't go off the deep end," Conrad said. "We need you to stay focused and tell us what happened."

"You're right." She walked to the sofa and sat.

"Let me think. OK. You guys left and we were hanging around. I started telling her about the history of my house." She looked at Maria. "It was a stop on the underground railroad."

Maria nodded.

"I told her about the secret tunnel. And, of course, she wanted to see it." She jumped up. "That's it, the secret tunnel. I was showing it to her when I heard a noise. I told her to stay put while I checked it out. I came out here and...a man." She pointed at the sliding door in the dining room. "He was over there. We struggled. He must have hit me in the head."

"Did you recognize the man, Zink?" Conrad's voice was urgent.

"It was the man from the flower shop. David Hamm."

"You're sure it wasn't Raymond?" Maria asked.

"It wasn't Raymond. It was definitely the man from the flower shop."

"Why would he want Layla? I don't even know him. Why would he take my child?" Her voice trembled and she knew she was close to hysteria again. She swallowed it down.

Conrad put a comforting hand on her arm. "Where's the secret tunnel, Suzanne?"

"I didn't know you had a secret tunnel," the chief said.

"I was afraid the historical society would come in and take over my house, so I didn't tell anybody about it." She tilted her head towards a door in the kitchen. "It's in the basement."

"Zink, you need to go to the hospital." The EMS worker moved towards Suzanne. "You've probably got a concussion. I gave you time to tell your story, but now it's time to go to the hospital."

"Forget it. I'm not going anywhere. Layla went missing on my watch and I'm going to find her."

"I'll make sure she gets to the hospital later." Chief Martin stepped between Zink and the EMS guy. "I promise. Thanks for your help."

Suzanne led the way down the basement steps. She pulled on a string at the bottom of the basement. A single bare light bulb lit up the dark. It was an old dirt basement. Not much more than a hole dug out of the ground.

Maria's gaze searched the ceilings. There had to be spiders up there somewhere. Exposed pipes and rafters were the only decoration.

"Not much to look at." Suzanne led the group to a bookcase. "We were standing here talking about the tunnel. I heard a noise upstairs. I told her to wait here while I checked it out."

"Is there another way out of here besides the way we came?" Conrad asked.

"Only the tunnel, but I didn't even have time to show it to her before I went back up the steps." She bent down and poked through the shelves to a hole in the dirt wall. "That's the tunnel."

"Did you show her where the tunnel was, Suzanne?" Conrad asked.

"I never moved the shelf, but I pointed at it. We were talking about it, and I was getting ready to move the shelf out of the way when I heard the noise. I told Layla to wait here until I got back." Suzanne closed her eyes. "Thank God I did. I didn't really think anything was wrong. Just figured it was the cat that came in. The alarm system should have gone off if the perimeter was breached. It didn't."

"Layla called me with your cell phone."

"I gave it to her while I went upstairs."

Maria paced around the room looking for other hiding spots.

"But if you never moved the shelf, then she didn't leave through the tunnel." Chief Martin said.

"That's not necessarily true." Conrad bent down.

"What do you mean?"

Conrad pointed through the shelving. "No back. It was open. Layla's small enough, she might have crawled through the hole."

Maria stared into the black hole.

Had Layla climbed through the shelf and the hole? To safety?

"She might have heard the scuffle upstairs and got scared. I've been teaching her to hide if she thought a bad man was chasing her. Where does this lead?"

Suzanne's voice was grim. "About a half-mile into the woods."

"I'm going to crawl through here," Chief Martin said. "Conrad, call dispatch and tell them to contact the search and rescue dog people."

"You can't get in there." Suzanne protested. "In case you haven't noticed, you've put on a few pounds in the past few years. I'll do it, chief."

"It's dark." Maria had to work to keep the tremble out of her voice. "We need to find her. She's probably so scared."

"There's no way you're going in there." Conrad's voice was firm. "You've probably got a concussion, Zink. You've got no business crawling around in there. If you pass out again, that's going to be a bigger problem. I'll go."

Maria shook her head. "I'll go." She held up a

hand to ward off their protests. "I know I'm not a policeman, but she's my daughter, and I'm the smallest. No arguing."

"She's right." Conrad nodded.

"Anybody have a flashlight?"

36

Maria crawled into the space trying not to think about spiders, bugs, or the rats that might be using the tunnel as home. *Think about Layla.* That was the only thing that mattered.

In one hand she held the flashlight. The other hand she used to brush away dirt as she moved through the tunnel. As she slithered through, she couldn't help but wonder how the escaping male slaves had managed. The tunnel was so tight.

A bright narrow beam lit her path. Several inches ahead, she saw something. Not Layla, but a small black object. When she reached it, her fingers curled around it.

Suzanne's cell phone. Layla must have dropped it after the phone call. That's why she hadn't answered. As Maria picked up the phone a spider fell on her hand.

Her pulse jumped and she closed her eyes. *It's only a spider.* She resisted the urge to fling it. Instead, she calmly moved her hand to the side and waited as it skittered away.

After some maneuvering, she managed to get the cell phone in her pants pocket. Then she scooted and slithered her way through the tunnel once more. The tunnel narrowed, pushing against her, suffocating her. Her heart raced.

With God, all things are possible.

Even crawling through this horrible place. She could do it because she had to. Just as those slaves from long ago did. They slid through the narrow opening, hoping and praying for freedom. When they'd gotten to the end of the tunnel had their dreams ended, or were they successful?

She opened her eyes. Her gaze fell on another object. She scooted towards it. When she picked it up, her heart skipped a beat.

A man's watch.

Her heart plummeted. Someone had followed Layla.

Maria wiped a speck of dirt out of her eye and sniffed. Fresh air. Almost to the end and no Layla. Maybe Conrad and Suzanne had found Layla on the other side of the tunnel and Maria would be greeted with a hug from her precious daughter.

She scooted faster, dirt falling in her hair and eyes. She had to find Layla before the man did.

She yelled, "Hello."

"We're here, Maria." It was Conrad.

"Is Layla with you? Did you find her?" There was a moment of hope, but then silence. She knew the answer to her question.

"Not yet, but we're looking." Conrad again tried to sound upbeat and encouraging.

The angle of her crawling shifted ever so slightly. She moved upwards towards the fresh air.

And then Conrad was above. His arms reached down and lifted her out. She leaned against him for a moment. He brushed the dirt from her hair. Then she stepped back from him.

Suzanne, Chief Martin, and three other officers were there—the entire Sunberry police force.

But no Layla.

Maria fought back the tears.

She handed the items from the tunnel to Conrad. "I found Suzanne's cell phone and a man's watch. He must have followed her into the tunnel." The thought of some man chasing Layla through that tunnel chilled Maria to the bone. Her gaze moved through the trees.

Almost completely dark. Her poor baby was out there—afraid and alone.

Ben Martin examined the watch as Conrad held a flashlight up. "It hasn't been in the tunnel long. It's still working."

"We've got to find her." Maria wrung her hands together.

"The dogs won't be here for another hour or so," Ben explained.

"We can't wait that long." Conrad took charge. "Everyone, separate and start searching. Maria, you stay with me."

"Why?" It made more sense for everyone to be hunting in different areas. The quicker they searched the area, the quicker they would find Layla.

"Because you aren't armed." His words knocked the argument out of her.

She nodded.

Chief Martin motioned for them to go. "I'll be looking in a minute. I'm calling the State Police. It won't take long to get reinforcements here. Everyone get moving and keep your radios on."

"Come on, let's go find Layla." Conrad touched her arm, leading her away.

They moved through the darkened woods. Each shadow, each noise felt like a threat. Tears blurred her vision but didn't stop her from moving, from searching.

Conrad was close beside her. His presence calmed her.

"Should I call her?" Maria asked.

"Sounds like a good idea to me."

Her voice grew hoarse as she yelled out her daughter's name again and again.

Layla didn't answer.

"Oh, my gosh. I'm so stupid." Maria couldn't believe she'd forgotten.

"This isn't your fault."

"No, no, no. It's not that. The tracker. In my panic, I forgot all about it. There's a tracking device in Layla's purse."

"That's great news. If she has it on her, we can find her." Laughing, he hugged her. "What do you use to track it?"

"My cell phone."

"Where's your cell phone?"

"In your car, I guess. That's the last time I remember having it."

"Let's go." He grabbed her hand and they jogged through the trees towards Suzanne's house.

Ben Martin stood near the exit of the tunnel. "What's going on?"

"Maria has a tracking app on her cell phone for Layla."

"Where's the tracking device on Layla?"

"In her purse." Maria answered. "She carries it everywhere with her."

"So, if she still has it, we can find her." Chief Martin nodded.

"Exactly," Conrad said.

"She never goes anywhere without her little pink

purse."

"OK, I'll be here, coordinating the search. Keep me informed."

Maria clung to Conrad's hand, her heart bursting with hope.

God was with them, as always. She just needed to remember that.

37

Maria's purse lay on the floor of the cruiser. She rummaged through it until she found the cell phone. Her finger quickly pressed on the app icon.

The signal finally flashed.

She pressed some buttons. "It looks like she's behind the house. In the woods. All we have to do is follow the red line." She held the phone up to Conrad.

"Is she moving?"

"No. Do you...think there's...why isn't she moving. She might be hurt."

"It doesn't mean anything. All it means is she's hiding somewhere, and that's a good thing."

His words were meant to reassure her, but even as she nodded, other possibilities crowded in.

"May I?" Conrad put a hand out for her phone. As he moved towards the woods, he handed her his cell phone. "Hit number one. It's the chief's number. Tell him what we're doing."

By the time she hung up, they were at the edge of the woods once again. She turned on the flashlight to light the way.

A moment later they were joined by Chief Martin and Suzanne.

No one spoke as they followed Conrad. They passed the tunnel exit and walked farther into the towering trees.

"Almost there," Conrad announced.

Please let her be there. Maria walked faster as she attempted to keep pace with Conrad.

He stopped.

Her stomach lurched.

Nothing but trees and bushes. No Layla.

"Call her," Conrad said.

"Layla. Mommy's here. You can come out now. It's safe."

Nobody even breathed as they waited for a response. The seconds ticked by. Nothing.

Maria called again—louder.

Still no Layla.

Suzanne dropped to her knees. "The signal says she's here. She's got to be here." She started crawling. The flashlight lit her way.

Maria dropped to her knees and did the same.

In moments, beacons of lights lit up the ground as each of them crawled through the leaves searching for Layla.

38

"Found it," Ben Martin yelled out from a bush he'd crawled into.

Maria's heart leapt for joy, but it was short-lived. "Let me see."

His hand came out of the bush holding a pink purse.

"Noooo," Maria moaned.

The tracking device hadn't kept Layla safe. Maria had failed.

Conrad put an arm around her shoulders, his strength holding her upright.

Her own strength was gone. "She would never leave without it. Not willingly. She knew it was important to keep with her at all times."

"Don't jump to conclusions." Conrad squeezed her shoulder. "Don't panic. We're going to find her. I promised you that, and I always keep my promises."

"I need some light here." Chief Martin was still in the bush.

All the flashlights turned in his direction.

Ben crawled out and stood up. He brushed the dirt off his pants. "It looks as if she might have been hiding in there. But it doesn't look like a struggle. She must have gone with him willingly."

Maria closed her eyes. The ground swayed and she couldn't breathe.

Layla wouldn't go with a stranger willingly. That

meant only one thing.

Raymond.

Her faith wavered. She would never see her daughter again.

The monster would make sure of that. Embers of hatred sparked in her heart.

Conrad's arms went around her. "God's in control, Maria. Not Raymond."

She leaned against him. In a whisper, she said, "Pray for Layla."

Softly, Conrad's words flowed from his mouth to Maria's ears and to God. The red embers flickered and then cooled. She would not let Raymond destroy her relationship with God.

Conrad's arms remained firmly around her, supporting her. It was the only thing that kept her from collapsing. His voice was strong—commanding—keeping her grounded. "Maria, you can't fall apart now. Layla needs you. Take some deep breaths."

Layla needs you. The words sank in, and she knew Conrad was right. She leaned over and sucked in deep breaths. "You're right. I can't fall apart now." She stood up, grim determination in her mind.

They would find Layla.

39

The black night sky turned a smoky gray as morning broke. Maria sat in a chair that some nameless person provided. She'd lost track of time as she waited.

Layla was gone.

She stared off into the foggy horizon. Her mind was numb and her spirit deflated. Without Layla, her life had no meaning. Why would God let her baby be taken from her—again? She trembled.

Conrad's hand touched her shoulder. "Are you cold, Maria?"

She shook her head.

A moment later, he draped a blanket from the cruiser around her shoulders. He leaned down close to her. "We're going to find her, Maria. You've got to have faith."

"She's gone. I know it."

Suzanne stood on the other side. "Don't stop believing, Maria. If you stop hoping, then you stop living. This is only the beginning of the search, not the end."

Tears filled Maria's eyes, grateful for these people who were willing to help her find Layla.

Suzanne looked at Conrad. "I've got an idea."

****

"All done." Conrad hit the send button on the

computer.

The three of them were back at the Sunberry Police Department. The search for the news reporter's murderer continued, but it did so without them.

"Do you think this will work?" Maria asked.

He didn't have high hopes.

Zink nodded. "I think it will. It's the only lead we have. David Hamm must be involved. And weren't we blessed to have the license plate number on his rental along with his picture?"

Of course, he might not be driving the same car any longer, but Conrad didn't tell them that.

Zink continued. "And it's being sent out to every police department in the state right now."

"So what happens with it?" Maria asked.

"It works a little different than an Amber Alert, and we don't have as much red tape to go through. Along with TV and radio stations, it gets emailed out to anyone who's signed up to be notified."

"Like who?"

"Bus and taxi companies, gas stations and other stores subscribe to it. Of course, this is only statewide so..." Suzanne shrugged. "But it's been very effective in the six months it's been in place."

"Good."

"Now, it's just a matter of waiting." Conrad looked at Maria.

She seemed almost zombie-like.

"You must be exhausted. Would you like to lie down for a while?"

"While Layla's with that...that monster? Not likely."

****

Maria sat staring at the wall. She should never have come back to Sunberry. The mistake had cost Layla dearly.

"Maria." Conrad put a comforting arm on her back. "There's nothing more to do here. Where would you like to go?" Conrad must be exhausted.

"You're giving up?"

"Of course not. But she's not here, so there's no reason to stay. You are worn out. Time for you to get some rest."

Tears fell down her cheeks. "This is my fault."

"It is not your fault. And we're going to find Layla. I'm not giving up until I bring her home to you. And I don't want you to give up, either." He picked up her hand. "We'll get through this together. I promise."

"I believe you." She took a deep breath and gazed at him. He was a strong man. And she had God on her side, too.

His hand brushed her cheek. "Good. Now where would you like to go? Back to your apartment? To a hotel?"

"She's not going anywhere." Suzanne walked up to them. "Except to my house. You can stay with me. There's no reason for you to be alone right now."

"I can't impose."

"You're not. I want you there. You can't go back your apartment. It would only drive you crazy. Believe me, I know. I'll take your keys and get you some fresh clothes and anything else you want. OK?"

Maria nodded, not really caring where she was or what she did.

40

Three days passed without a break in the case.

Layla had simply vanished.

Maria was sure she would lose her mind those first few days.

The FBI and the U.S. Marshals assured her Raymond was dead, but she refused to believe them.

Raymond had managed to get her daughter out of the country.

She would never see Layla again. It was time to do something. Maria sat up in bed. She was still staying with Suzanne, but she couldn't stay there forever. She didn't know what to do or where to go. Without Layla she had no reason to be any specific place.

But Layla was alive—somewhere.

"Knock, knock." Suzanne opened the door. She held a cup of coffee in her hand. "Rise and shine. Time to get up and get on with living, Maria."

"I can't."

"I know it's hard."

"You don't know anything." Bitterness tinged her voice.

"Yes, I do know." Suzanne sat on the bed beside her. "You have to get up and keep living. You can't lie in bed forever."

"You don't understand."

"Oh, believe me, I do." Her eyes met Maria's. "I have a son."

"What do you mean you have a son? Where is he?"

"His father kidnapped him two years ago. I haven't seen him since. We're looking for him, but so far nothing."

Her mind flashed to the child's room. "Oh, Suzanne. I...I...didn't know. And then two missing children. It must have been a nightmare for you."

"It has been. There are days I think I can't make it through, but I do. And so will you."

"But how? Why? What's the point?"

"The point is that someday I'm going to find my son, and when I do, I want to have a life for him to come back to. And besides, God gives each of us the gift of life. We dishonor him if we waste it."

Dishonor God. That wasn't what she intended to do, but... "God certainly doesn't expect me to go on as if nothing happened."

"He doesn't, but He does expect you to have faith. And to get out of that bed."

"I don't know how to live without Layla."

Tears glistened in Suzanne's eyes. "One step at a time. One breath at a time. One minute at a time. That's all you can do."

"How old is he?"

"He's four now. He was two when his father took him."

"Why did he do that?"

"Because he was about to be arrested for embezzlement. Instead, he took the money and Andrew and disappeared."

"I am so sorry, Suzanne."

"I fell apart at first. But I knew if I gave up and gave in to the grief, the terror, the emptiness, then I would have nothing left to give Andrew when he comes back. So, as hard as it is, I get up every day and live my life."

Maria looked at Suzanne through new eyes. She'd liked her before. Now she admired the woman a lot more, knowing the circumstances in which Suzanne worked every day.

"Andrew and Michael are being looked for by the FBI, and one of these days we're going to find them and I'll have my son back." She patted Maria's hand. "Just the way you'll get Layla back. In the meantime, you can't give up."

"So…it's time to get up and get moving."

"That's what I'm saying, girl. And besides…you've got some company."

****

After a quick shower, Maria walked into Suzanne's living room.

Conrad sat on the sofa talking with a young blonde girl.

Two sets of eyes turned in her direction.

The teen-aged girl she'd offered a job earlier in the week. Had it been less than a week? She hadn't even thought about The Bouquet in light of all that had happened.

The young girl stood, clearly uncomfortable. "I'm so sorry. I didn't know anything about what's been going on. I don't have a TV at home. I didn't know. I showed up at your flower shop to work, and then he brought me here. I tried to tell him I'd just go home, but he insisted I come."

Maria's mind flashed back to the day she told the

girl to come work at the flower shop.

Layla had been aggravated that someone was trying to take away her job.

Tears welled up, but Maria refused to give in to them.

Honor God.

That's what Suzanne did by going to work every day, and that's what Maria would do as well.

She looked at Conrad. He winked at her.

She shook her head and rewarded him with a slight smile. "Don't think I don't know what you're doing, Conrad. This is just a ploy."

"Me? All I did was bring your new employee to see you."

She ran a hand through her still damp hair. *Could she do this? Did she even want to?* Her cover had been blown. Witness Protection wanted to move her to a new location, but there was no way she was leaving Sunberry until Layla...was back. "I'm...I'm not ready."

"I know. I'm sorry. I didn't mean to intrude. I'm so sorry." The girl wrung her hands.

"Yes, you are, Maria." Conrad said. "You are stronger than you give yourself credit for."

"I ca—oh, no. I just remembered I have a wedding this afternoon. I've done nothing for it. I didn't even call to cancel."

"Good thing you have Rose here to help. And what a great name for someone working in a flower shop, don't you think?"

"Your name is Rose?" Maria asked.

"It is, but most people call me Rosie."

"That's pretty. Write down your phone number and if I open up again, I'll give you a call, Rosie."

"We don't have a phone. I didn't mean to cause no

problem. Don't worry about it."

"I'm sorry." Maria looked at Conrad. "I just can't do it. I'm not ready."

"OK, you'll be ready when you're ready. I'll drive Rosie home, and then I'll be back. I'm off work today."

She'd disappointed Conrad and Suzanne.

Honor God. Keep your promises.

It was only a small wedding with a few flower arrangements and the bridal bouquet. Maria stared past Rosie, thinking of the bride who would have no bridal bouquet as she marched down the aisle that afternoon on her father's arm. She threw up her hands in surrender. "Never mind. She can come to The Bouquet with me. I've got a wedding to do. But first I'll need to drive into Columbus to the Floral Warehouse."

A big smile landed on Conrad's face.

****

Maria put the final arrangement in her floral truck and turned to a smiling Conrad and Rosie. "I can't believe we actually finished with time to spare."

"That bride will be very happy," Conrad said.

"Thanks to both of you. I could never have finished without your help."

"Don't forget about me." Suzanne walked out of the back. "If I hadn't got your van at your apartment, all your hard work would be for naught."

"So true. So true." Conrad chimed in. "And, I'm sure you stopped in to check on Mr. Ricky Snyder while you were there."

"I did no such thing."

"Thanks," Maria hugged Suzanne. "I couldn't have made it through this week without you."

Suzanne hugged her back and whispered in her ear. "You've honored God today."

Maria turned to Conrad. His arms went around her and she relaxed for a moment, but then pulled away, smiling. "Who would ever have thought a tough cop like you could make such beautiful flower arrangements?"

"I am a man of many talents."

"Yes, you are. Thanks so much—for everything." She looked at her two new friends. "I don't know how to repay you."

"I don't know about Zink," Conrad said, "but you can buy me dinner tonight."

"It's a date." Her cheeks turned warm. "I don't mean a *date* date. I just meant it's a...a...dinner."

"It's a date. See you then." He winked.

41

Rosie sat beside Maria in the back of the church.

People crowded in around the bride and groom, laughing, hugging and congratulating the newlyweds who still stood at the front of the church. No formalities here, no receiving line, just joyful celebration.

"Beautiful wedding, don't you think?" Maria whispered.

The bride had been so grateful for Maria providing the flowers in spite of her circumstances. She'd insisted Maria and Rosie stay for the wedding.

"It was. You could see the love on their faces. No wonder you love your job. Flowers make people happy."

"Most of the time." Maria didn't mention that flowers were part of the funeral ritual as well. "Ready to go?"

"Sure."

"How did you get to The Bouquet?" Maria asked, once they were in the car. "Is your car there?"

"I don't have a car. I walked."

"I'll drop you off at your house."

"You don't have to do that. I can walk. It's not that far."

"It's not a bother. Where do you live?"

Rosie's cheeks turned pink. "It's outside of town. My mom and I live in one of the rooms at the Dew

Drop Inn."

"Never heard of it."

"It's just a tiny motel. Not very nice, but it's all we can afford for now."

"I'm sure it's fine."

"It's horrible actually." Rosie shrugged. "But my mom's sick and can't work right now. We're blessed to have a roof over our head."

"I'm so sorry." Maria was glad she'd offered Rosie a job. She reached in her purse and pulled out three twenties. "For today's work."

"That's too much."

"Not for today. It was special circumstances. From now on, I'll make sure to pay you on time. How's that sound?"

Rosie nodded and took the money. "Can we stop at the grocery store before you take me out? That way I can pick up some food. And maybe some orange juice for my mom. It might make her feel better."

"Great idea. I need a few things, as well. I'm planning to go back to my own apartment tonight." She bit her lip at the thought of the empty home, but Suzanne was right. She couldn't go to bed and give up.

Honor God would be her mantra for now.

She'd taken steps today to reclaim her life, and in the process made two people's lives a little better. Four, if she counted Rosie and her mother.

42

"Do you think we did the right thing?" Conrad looked up from his computer screen at Zink. In spite of not being scheduled, they'd both ended up at the station, trying to find a lead on Layla.

"You mean getting Maria up out of bed and back to the flower shop?"

"It might be too soon. It's only been a few days. She has a right to a meltdown. Her daughter's missing."

"She does have a right, but believe me. It won't do her any good. It will only make things worse. The longer she was in the bed the harder it would have been to get up and take that first step."

"It's amazing how you come in each day and smile."

Zink brushed her fingernails against her chest and smiled. "I am sort of amazing, aren't I?"

"Don't let it go to your head."

She leaned back in her chair and twirled a pencil. "I do think it's the right thing for Maria to do. As my therapist explained, people are creatures of habit, so if we get in the habit of giving up and being depressed, we only dig a deeper hole to climb out of."

"So, the reverse is true as well."

Zink looked at him with a question in her eyes.

"If you get in the habit of ignoring the bad things, it makes it easier to get on with life."

"I have found that to be true."

"The U.S. Marshals aren't very happy about her decision to stay in town."

"Well they're idiots if they thought Maria would just pack up and leave for parts unknown without her daughter. So she might as well forge some sort of life here until..." She changed the subject. "I hear that Morgan Reed resigned."

"Resigned? I doubt it. More like got fired. I can't believe she was just going to turn Maria over to the Feds without an argument."

"I don't think she's in any danger now, anyway."

"Who? Morgan?"

She wadded up a sheet of paper and threw it at him. "No, not Morgan. Maria. Whoever took Layla clearly wanted her and not Maria. I think she's safe."

"For what it's worth, I agree."

His computer beeped an alarm message. After clicking a few keystrokes, he looked up at Zink again. "They found Hamm's rental car."

"Really? Where?"

"At the car rental place where it was rented from. One of the workers was checking out another car and found it."

"You're kidding me. That's an odd thing to do."

"It is. What do you suppose it means?"

Neither of them spoke for a few minutes as they each worked out what it could mean.

"If I had a guess," Zink finally said, "I would say it means he dropped it off and hopped on a plane."

"With Layla?"

"That would be hard to do, wouldn't it? He would need ID for her to get on a plane. Maybe he was alone."

Conrad refused to believe the worst. Why would the man have gone to all the trouble of taking the little girl and then kill her? It didn't make sense. "Maybe he stole another car. He knew we'd be looking for that one so he had to ditch it and get something else. If he took a car out of long-term parking, it could be days or weeks before the owner even knows it's been stolen."

"Yeah, it would be like trying to find a needle in a haystack. Except we don't even know what the needle looks like. Not good."

"Not good at all." He stood and picked up his keys.

"Where are you going?"

"To talk to the guy who found the car."

Zink tapped her watch. "Maria will be here to pick you up for your date."

"I think finding her daughter is more important than missing a dinner date."

"I do too, but you should call and let her know you might be late. After all, it's your first date."

"Not if you count the coffee dates we had. And besides you heard the woman. It's not a *date* date, anyway."

"Oh, please. The two of you are so smitten."

"All the more reason to find her daughter. I don't see much happening in our relationship while her heart is broken. Anyway, I'll leave a message here and tell her I'll be a little late."

"Are you going to tell her what you're doing?"

"No reason to get her hopes up."

****

Maria pulled into the parking lot of the

ramshackle motel. It was worse than she imagined. She glanced over at Rosie.

"I know it looks bad." She shrugged. "Who am I kidding? It is what it is."

Maria was glad she'd offered help to the teen. "How much is it?"

"Seventy-five dollars a week. That takes about half my mom's check, and then we use the rest for food."

"Are you going to school?"

"I am. I know I have to. It's the only way we're going to get out of this mess."

"Good girl." Making a decision, Maria looked over at Rosie. "I can give you twenty hours a week. Come in Wednesday after school and we can work out a schedule."

"Thanks. That will help so much."

Maria scanned the empty parking lot wondering if it was safe for Rosie and her mother. The place looked less than reputable. "Who else stays here?"

Rosie pointed at the first room. "Bob, that's the owner, stays there with his girlfriend. And then it was just Mom and me. We're in the second unit. But some guy showed up a few days ago. He stays in the last room. He gives me the creeps."

Her mother alarm went off. "Why?"

"I don't know. Something about him I don't like. Bob told me that he asked to have the very last room. Even though it's smaller than the rest of the rooms. And he keeps his car parked around back. Kind of strange since his car's the only one in the parking lot besides Bob's."

"Probably hiding from his wife or girlfriend?"

Rosie giggled. "Or both. You're probably right. We don't see that many people around here like him. I guess I'm just being judgmental because of his accent."

"His accent?" Maria's heart dropped a beat. *His accent.* Her world tilted on its axis. It wouldn't realign until she had Layla back.

A memory surfaced. Maria had been cooking Raymond's breakfast omelet. He'd walked in and smiled pleasantly at her. "How are you this morning, dear?" His voice sounded different somehow. She thought she was tired because sleep had not come easy for her the night before.

"Fine." She set down the plate in front of him. "And yourself?"

"Just wonderful. It looks delicious. So, what are your plans for today?"

His voice definitely sounded different. Raymond rarely engaged in morning conversation. And he never asked about her daily plans unless it related to Layla.

"Not much. I might take Layla to the park. And then we have swimming lessons this afternoon. I still have a few last-minute things to do for the benefit."

"That sounds nice. I read a newspaper article that said American children don't get as much physical activity as they need. We don't want our daughter to get fat and lazy, do we?"

Maria looked over at her husband. Had there been an odd tone when he said the word American? Almost a sneer. She chuckled. "I'm sure that's very true. So many children want to stay in the house playing video games for hours and hours instead of going outside in the fresh air."

"It is very sad indeed." His voice—clipped and stilted, almost a foreign accent, but that was impossible. He didn't speak with an accent. He was American.

She looked up from the omelet and over at him.

They gazes met.

He smiled, but it didn't reach his eyes.

A chill travelled down her spine.

They stared at each for a moment, and then he lifted the paper once again.

Maria turned back to the sink...

She'd ignored that moment so long ago and had regretted it ever since. She wouldn't ignore this moment. She looked over at Rosie. "What does this man look like?"

43

Rosie walked to the motel door. The girl turned and gave Maria a little wave, and then disappeared inside.

Maria's heart pounded, her anxiety rising. She had to find out who the stranger with the accent was in that motel room. She knew her thoughts were irrational and crazy, but so be it.

Putting her car into reverse she turned around. Rosie said the man parked his car behind the motel, but it would look too suspicious for her to drive behind the motel to get a look.

The last thing she wanted was to do something that would make him leave or cause him to be suspicious.

Her gaze scanned the area as her mind puzzled out her next move. The trees. The trees would hide her.

At the drive, she turned right instead of left towards town. She drove down the country road until she was out of sight of the motel, and then pulled to the side of the road.

Stepping out of the car, she stared at the woods. Were these the same woods that were behind Suzanne's house? They could be, but not knowing the area very well, she couldn't be sure.

Her mind's eye saw a man grabbing Layla as she made her way out of the tunnel and dragging her through the woods to the tiny motel. That would explain why they hadn't found a car. It could have been parked here at the motel the whole time. Layla here at the motel? So close to her all this time?

Maria fought back the rising emotions. This was not the time to fall apart.

But why was he still here, and was Layla really with him—if it was Raymond at all? It didn't make sense that he'd be here after almost a week. She was sure she was wrong, but she had to know for certain that the man in that motel room wasn't Raymond.

Instead of walking down the road, she headed into the trees. It felt safer—less exposed. With each step her heart pounded harder. One moment she knew she was right and in the next she knew she was being ridiculous and crazy. She stopped at the edge of the trees and stared at the motel.

Was Raymond in that room with Layla?

44

The car was parked behind the motel just as Rosie had described. Maria maneuvered to the best location, pulled out her cell phone, and took a picture of the car. But it was too far away.

She stepped further back into the woods.

Just in case someone was looking out the window.

She adjusted the picture making it larger and larger until she could read the license plate easily. Time to call Conrad.

She hit his number and waited. He would think she was nuts, and she probably was. But when Rosie said the words—man with an accent—something told her to listen and to act. No, not something—God.

"Hello, Maria. Did you get my message?"

"No, what message?"

"I left a message at the station telling you I'd be late. Isn't that why you're calling?"

"I'm not at the station. I need a favor."

"You name it."

"I need you to run a license plate for me." A long pause. "Did you hear me?"

"I did. But it surprised me. Why do you need it?"

"I'd rather not tell you. It's sort of crazy. But I've got to find out who owns this car."

"Not a problem. I'll be glad to do it. Go ahead and give me the number." Conrad's voice was calm and reassuring. He didn't sound as if he thought she was nuts. After she'd given him the number, he said, "I'll call you back in a minute."

****

Zink stared at him with a question in her eyes. "What's going on?"

She was driving them back from the car rental agency. It had been a wasted trip.

"I'm not sure. Maria wants me to find out who a car belongs to."

"That's odd. What does she need it for?"

"She didn't tell me that part."

"You should have asked. It has to be about Layla. What else could it be?"

"Do you think?"

"Sarcasm isn't necessary."

He hit some keys on the inboard netbook. "Interesting. The car is registered to a Hannah Dunnlevy from Wooster."

"Now, why would she want to know about some woman's car from Wooster?"

He hit numbers on his cell. "I don't know, but I'm going to give this Hannah a quick call." He spoke into the phone for a few moments, hung up and looked at Zink. "I think Maria just found our needle in a haystack."

45

Maria clicked the phone to off. Using the tree as an anchor, she sat down. The bark pressed into her back. From this vantage point, she had an unobstructed view of the car.

Conrad and Suzanne would be here soon. All she had to do was watch the car, make sure it didn't leave. But what if he left on foot and she didn't see him? What if the man slipped out the front door and walked away—with Layla.

Maria sent a prayer up to God, thanking Him for putting woods around three sides of the motel. She walked through the trees, checking for other doors on the ramshackle motel. There were none. She let out her breath. Now, she had to get back and watch the car.

She could hide in the forest at an angle where she could see the front door and with just a few steps, she could move to check on the car every few minutes. For now, she'd watch the front door, because she'd hear if someone started the car.

Sticks crunched beneath her feet and the car came back into sight. Her mind raced faster than her pulse.

Craziness was winning.

Be still and know that I am God.

She leaned against a tree, her breath ragged. When her breathing slowed and sanity returned, she moved closer to the edge of the woods. Her gaze focused on the door.

It opened. A man walked out.

A small sob escaped.

Not Raymond. Her crazy thoughts were just that. Crazy. Whoever this man was, it wasn't Raymond and had nothing to do with Layla.

She wiped away a tear. At least she knew now. There'd been no way she could have left without seeing the man with the accent.

Her body sagged against the tree from emotional exhaustion. Maria watched as he looked around, and then went behind the motel.

The man in the alley?

Her pulse ramped up once again. It was too far away to be sure, but he certainly looked like the man with the gun—same body type—dark hair—dark skin. It could be him. Was he leaving? She looked at her watch.

Conrad had said it would take them a while to get to her.

She couldn't just let the man leave. The more she watched him, she was almost positive it was the man from the alley—or at least it could possibly be. Should she get her car so she could follow him, if necessary?

Not a good idea. Her car was too far away and besides, if she left she wouldn't see what direction he went.

He reappeared and went back into the motel.

She moved at an angle to check on the car. The trunk was open. She moved closer, careful to stay out of sight.

He came back out carrying something in his arms.

A bundle that could be a child? Layla?

Maria's mouth turned to sand and her body trembled. Help me, God. She forced herself to breathe.

He placed it in the trunk, and then looked around for a moment before he closed the lid and walked back to the motel room.

Waiting until he disappeared, she sprinted towards the car, thankful for all those hours of running and training. She'd kept in shape, worried about the need to stay ahead of anyone after them. She moved to the driver's side and released the trunk latch. She ran to the back of the car and lifted the trunk lid.

In the darkened corner Layla huddled, wrapped in a blanket, still and unmoving.

She gasped. Her arms reached for her daughter.

A sound came from behind her.

But before she could turn, something hit her on the head.

She struggled to stay standing, but darkness came.

Betrayed

46

Zink pulled into the rundown motel's parking lot. "I can't believe Rosie and her mother live in this place. I thought it closed down years ago."

"It did. I'm sure it's not licensed. But we'll deal with that later. Let's go to the back and find the car. Then we can check out the motel room if Maria hasn't already broken in."

"She promised you that she'd wait. I'm sure she will."

Zink maneuvered around potholes and gaps that threatened to swallow the cruiser.

He held his tongue even though he wanted to urge her to go faster. As they turned the corner of the building, he sighed.

The back parking lot was empty.

"Now what?" Zink stepped on the brake but kept the car idling.

"Go to the front and I'll call Maria. She probably saw him leave."

He hit redial. The phone rang. No answer. "She's not answering."

"I'm going to knock on the door." Zink opened the door and stepped out.

"Fine, I'll try her number again."

No one answered. He got out and headed to the motel office with a sinking feeling in the pit of his stomach.

A door opened and Rosie stepped out. Her eyes widened. "Mr. Travis, what are you doing here?"

"I don't have time to explain right now. Did you see the man in the end room leave?"

"Yeah about fifteen minutes ago."

"Did you see Maria with him?"

"No, she dropped me off a while ago and left. What's going on?"

"Where's the manager?"

She pointed to the first room.

He knocked. TV sounds came from inside but no one answered. He knocked again—louder. "Sunberry Police Department."

A moment later the door opened. A man in a dirty T-shirt stared at him. "You ain't got no jurisdiction here. I know my rights."

"You're right about that, buddy." Conrad forced his impatience down. "I'm not looking for a problem. I'm only here to check on the guy who rented that room down at the end."

After a long drag on his cigarette, the owner answered. "What about him?"

"What's his name?"

"Mr. Green." The man cackled. "He didn't give me a name and I didn't ask for one. He gave me cash and that was fine by me."

"I want in his room."

The man shrugged. "Whatever."

"Key."

He disappeared and a moment later, he handed Conrad the key. "If the dude comes back, I'm not getting involved between the two of yous. It's not my problem."

"Good thinking." Conrad walked towards the

other room.

Rosie jogged alongside him. "What's going on?"

"I don't have time right now, but you need to go in your room and stay there until I let you know it's safe to come out."

Her eyes widened. "Safe?"

He nodded.

She backtracked to her room.

47

Conrad stood in the middle of 'Mr. Green's' room holding a pair of girly, little pink shoes. He held them up as Zink walked into the room. "What are the chances these aren't Layla's?"

"Not much. I called Ben. He's notifying State Police. We have no jurisdiction out here."

"So I heard."

"There's a BOLO out for the car, and Ben's working on an Amber Alert. We'll find them."

"Find anything outside?"

She held up a purse. "It's Maria's. I found it against a tree. She must have sat down to wait and then..."

"She saw something that made her leave it."

"Like Layla."

"Now he has both of them. I suppose her cell phone's in her purse."

"It is. So we can't use it to track her."

"Great. Just great."

She put a hand on his arm. "At least she's most likely with Layla. I know that may not be comforting to you, but it is to her. Believe me. If I could be with Andrew, it wouldn't matter to me what the circumstances were."

****

Encased in darkness, Maria opened her eyes. The back of her head throbbed. Must be in the trunk. *Layla.* She reached out and encircled her little girl with her arms

Tears sprang to her eyes. "Oh, thank you, God. Thank you." She hugged Layla. With slow hands she inspected her daughter. There didn't seem to be any injuries.

Maria wiped at the tears as she felt the warmth of her little girl's body next to hers and heard the easy breathing. Her baby was only asleep.

Layla murmured and nestled in.

Maria untied her feet and arms. And gingerly took off the tape.

Layla stirred, but didn't wake.

They were moving.

The good news—it was a new model car, which meant there had to be a latch somewhere inside the trunk to open the lid from the inside.

The bad news—it was too dark to see where the latch might be.

48

Conrad stood to the side as State Police bagged and tagged the evidence. A BOLO was out on the stolen car.

The Bouquet's shop van had been found a half-mile down the road, but it held no clues as to where Maria had vanished.

Ben Martin walked into the room with a large African-American man. "This is Marcus Hanks, the FBI agent Maria told us about."

"Can we talk outside?" Conrad asked.

"Sure." Marcus's voice was deep.

The group walked outside.

Conrad took a deep appreciative breath of the fresh air. "So, you know Maria?"

The man nodded.

"Maria is convinced she's dealing with her husband—Rahmed Hamed. No matter how many people tell her he's dead and it's not possible, she won't believe them." Conrad stared at Marcus Hanks waiting for a response.

Marcus stared back without blinking. "Is there a question in there somewhere?"

Was the man playing mind games? Conrad was losing his patience. "You know there is. Is it possible? Is her husband still alive?"

Marcus sighed and looked up at the sky. His left hand straightened his gold earring. He looked back at

Conrad and their gazes locked. "I shot the man. That's what I can tell you. He looked dead the last time I saw him. Did I see him in a casket? No. On a gurney in a morgue? No, didn't see that, either. I'm beginning to wish I had."

"So he could be alive?"

"That's not what I was told. And I wouldn't know why my bosses would lie to me."

"You think you'd be the first man whose boss lied to him?" Conrad asked.

"Of course not, but why would they?"

"Who knows? Maybe the man escaped and they didn't want to admit to the world they'd lost a terrorist. Or crazy as it sounds, maybe he cooperated and they gave him his freedom as a reward."

Marcus shook his head and took several paces away from Conrad, but then turned back. "I hope that's not what happened."

****

Maria started softly touching the walls of her prison, hoping her movements were quiet. That emergency latch was in here somewhere.

"Mommy." Her daughter's voice was a whisper.

"Oh, Layla." Giving up her search, she put her arms around her daughter. "I love you."

"I knew you would find me, Mommy."

Her eyes filled with tears as she hugged Layla. "And I always will. Keep your voice down, sweetie. We don't want the man to hear us."

"OK."

"Did you see the man who took you, Layla?" Maria wasn't sure she was ready to hear the answer.

"Yes, he lied to me, Mommy. He said he'd take me to Daddy, but he didn't. He tied me up. He keeps making me drink stuff, and then I fall asleep." Layla's voice trembled. "I'm scared."

I am, too. "Did he hurt you?"

"No, Mommy. He just kept telling me Daddy was a hero and he was going to take me home. He made me drink something nasty."

"I'm so sorry."

"I'm scared."

"Me, too. But God is with us. And Mr. Conrad and Miss Suzanne are looking for us right this minute. It'll be OK." She squeezed her eyes shut, hoping she wasn't lying to her daughter. "Layla, there's some sort of latch or button that will open the trunk. We need to find it so that when he stops we can get out. Help me hunt for it."

"OK."

They untangled themselves from each other's arms.

"If you find it, don't press it. We don't want the trunk to fly open while we're driving down the highway." Even as she said the words, she wondered why not. If the trunk flew open, the man would have to stop to close it.

"Mommy. I think I found it."

"Where is it?"

Layla put her hand over her mother's and guided it.

"Great job, sweetie. And you know what? I've been thinking. Maybe we should hit the button now. The man will have to stop the car to put it down and that will be our chance to escape."

"That's a good idea, Mommy."

"OK, then. I want you to squeeze as far back as you can against the trunk. That way you'll be safe."

"You might fall out."

"That's not going to happen. I'll be very careful. Trust me." As she said the words, she remembered Conrad saying the same thing to her. "Now, what I want you to do is the very second the car stops, I want you to be ready to jump out and run. But we have to be careful of cars, in case we're on a highway."

"OK."

Maria was terrified, but it was the right choice. If she waited until the car came to a stop, it might be too late. And the element of surprise couldn't hurt. She had to try now. "Layla, when I tell you to run, you run. Don't worry about me. I'll—"

"No, I'm not leaving you." Her daughter's voice turned stubborn.

Maria made her own voice firm. "Oh, yes you are. And we're not arguing about it, Layla. You run as fast as you can and you run to the first store or business you see and have them call the police. I mean it, Layla. This is important."

"But—"

"And remember Sunberry Police. Conrad Travis. Got it?"

"OK."

"Say it."

"Sunberry Police. Conrad Travis."

"Good girl. Are you ready?"

****

Conrad sat at his desk in the Sunberry Police station, not believing what he was hearing.

"The prints belong to a Daoud Hamed, but he anglicized it to David Hamm." Marcus's face turned darker with anger and rage with each word he uttered. The man looked furious. "He has a student visa and—"

"Is that legal?" Ben Martin's red mustache twitched as he asked the question.

"What—to change his name?"

Ben nodded.

"All his forms show Daoud, and in parenthesis, David. I'm assuming his IDs show him as David, not that it matters."

"Why do you say that?" Conrad asked.

"Because he's here legally and he's been busy with college. According to his records, he attends his classes and is getting A's in all of them. We've got people on their way there now, so we'll know more once they talk with his associates. But for the moment, he looks like a typical graduate student. We had no idea he had any connection to Rahmed Ham—"

"Why not? That's the thing I don't get."

Marcus locked gazes with Conrad. "I am not the enemy. This wasn't my mistake. Hamed is a very common name in that part of the world and not every one of them are terrorists or even related to a terrorist. We can't refuse visas to every person with that last name."

Conrad wanted to argue but knew there wasn't much point. The only thing that mattered was finding Maria and Layla. "You admit there was a mistake."

Marcus nodded. "Oh, yeah, but I have nothing to do with student visas or monitoring the terrorist watch list."

"Sorry, I didn't mean to sound as if I was personally attacking you. I'm frustrated."

"We all are, buddy. They've been through enough."

Ben Martin stood up. "So, what are they telling you about Ramed Hamed? Is he dead or not?"

Marcus shrugged. "My boss assures me he's dead."

49

Maria waited as Layla got in position behind her.

Please, God. Keep her safe. Let this crazy idea work.

"I love you, Layla. When you get out, you run and don't look back. And remember—Sunberry Police, Conrad Travis." She pressed the button.

She smiled as she heard the release of the latch. Sunshine trickled in through the crack. She moved closer and peeked out through the tiny opening, but couldn't really see anything. Keeping her back pressed against Layla, she used her hands to push upwards on the trunk lid.

Her eyes squinted involuntarily at the sudden brightness.

Tires screeched.

She looked out. Not a highway. No other cars on the road. Still in the country somewhere. Maybe, she should have waited longer—listened for more traffic.

The car thudded to a stop as she was reaching for Layla. She lifted her little girl up and tossed her out. "Run, Layla, run. Fast."

Layla ran.

Maria climbed out of the trunk.

A man ran past her towards Layla.

Maria jumped on him.

He swung around to get her off.

She held on tighter, dragging her feet. Using both arms, he attempted to knock her off him. She held on as tightly as she could.

They both fell to the ground.

He struggled to get up, but she wouldn't let go.

He won't get Layla. He'll have to kill me first. She grabbed his hair and pulled.

He cursed at her and swung his fist, but she managed to duck away.

The two rolled around on the ground.

Her grasp was slipping. No, she couldn't let that happen.

He slid out of her hold and stood. Maria grabbed his leg, but he kicked her in the head and escaped again. Ignoring the pain, she jumped to her feet. When she closed the gap between them, she kicked him in the sensitive area where his thighs met his torso, just as her instructor had taught.

He doubled over with a moan, but didn't go down.

She grabbed his head and pushed him to the ground.

He swung at her and his fist connected with her face.

She hit the ground hard. Her vision blurred and stars exploded as she looked up.

He ran down the road. Towards Layla.

"No." She jumped up, but swayed. She ran after him, grabbing his arm when she got close enough. He pulled back his fist, but she head butted him in the stomach. The two toppled to the ground once again.

"You are a crazy woman," he screamed at her. "You have ruined everything."

She disentangled from him and ran after Layla. She'd only gone a few feet when the man yelled.

"Stop or I will shoot you."

She glanced back.

His gun was aimed at her.

A vehicle screeched to a stop near the car she'd escaped from.

Someone to help.

Forcing her legs to move, she ran past her attacker.

The gunshot rang out.

She moved towards the cars, praying.

"Help me. Call the police," she screamed at the driver of the other car

The door opened and a man stepped out.

50

Zink perched on her desk glaring at Marcus Hanks.

Conrad thought he cut an imposing figure and criminals probably gave up without a fight when they looked at the man.

Zink, on the other hand, didn't appear intimidated in the least. She put her hands on her hips. "This is all wonderful information. Of course, it would have been more helpful before he abducted Layla and her mother. I'm wondering how it helps us find them right now."

How had their peaceful little town become the hotbed for kidnappings and possible terrorist activity? If he'd read it in a novel, he'd have dismissed it as bizarre writing on the author's part. Apparently, truth really was stranger than fiction.

Nick Johns stepped from the dispatcher's tiny cubicle where he was pulling duty now that he was back from his family emergency. "Travis. Get in here. Now."

Conrad, shocked by Nick's tone, sat and stared. "Why?"

"Some girl's on the phone and won't speak to anyone but you."

He picked up the phone on his desk and punched the blinking button. "Hello."

"Mr. Conrad." A tiny voice spoke.

Layla. Still alive. Thank you, God.

"It's me. Is this Layla?"

"Yes, Mommy told me to call you."

"Is your mommy with you?"

"No." Her little voice trembled. "She told me to run and not wait for her. I didn't want to. I wanted her to come with me."

"You did the right thing, honey. Good for you for listening to your mommy. Where are you, Layla? I'll come and get you."

"I don't know."

"We're hiding in the back of my gas station." A man's voice came on the line. "I locked the door, but it's an old gas station. Not much security, I'm afraid. It won't stop anyone for long."

"Do you have a weapon?"

"It's in my hand as we speak."

"Good. Don't trust anyone unless the little girl says it's her mother. And whatever you do, don't listen if she says it's her father. Don't let a man take her. Whatever you do."

"Got it."

"Good man. What's your address?" He wrote it down and turned around and was face-to-face with Zink. Ben and Marcus pressed in against him on each side.

He explained as he pushed past them. "Gotta go."

He jogged out of the station and towards the cruiser.

Marcus ran past him blocking his way. "That's not your jurisdiction."

"I don't care whose jurisdiction it is. I'm getting that little girl and nobody's going to stop me. I made a promise to her mother, and I'm keeping it."

"I'm trying to tell you to take me with you. It's my jurisdiction."

51

Maria stared as he stepped out of the car.

Her heart stopped.

"Hello, Maria. You didn't expect to see me again, did you?"

Her mouth moved, but she couldn't form words. No matter how hard she struggled against it, he would win. She flinched as he grabbed her arm and twisted it.

"You keep causing problems for me. I'm getting very tired of it, Maria."

"Raymond." She gasped his name in spite of the pain travelling up her arm. She attempted to get away, but it only made the pain worse. Finally she found her voice. "They said I was wrong. That you were dead."

"I will deal with you later. Where is my daughter?" His voice shook with rage as he turned to the man scrambling to stand up. "Daoud, what happened?"

"Rahmed, my brother. It truly is you. I couldn't believe it when they told me you were alive."

"Where's my daughter?"

"That crazy woman opened the trunk while we were moving and she got away."

"Where's my daughter?" Raymond's voice was laced with fury.

The man he called Daoud pointed. "She couldn't have gotten that far. She's a little girl."

Raymond shoved Maria at the man. "Take care of

her. I'll go find Layla myself."

Maria ran towards Raymond. Every second she could delay him was one more second for Layla to get away from this monster. She kicked him in the back.

He fell forward and stumbled, but didn't fall. Turning quickly, Raymond grabbed her foot.

She fell to the ground. Gravel bit into her back, but she refused to give up.

Raymond's foot pressed against her chest. She struggled against the pain, barely able to breathe, but refused to let go.

"Shoot her. I don't have time for this. Shoot her, now." Raymond's voice was cold.

"I...I can't, Rahmed. I can't." Daoud stuttered and shook his head. "I can't. I made a vow not to kill again."

"Weakling. You are worthless. Just as Josef was. That was why he had to die."

"Josef? What do you mean?" The young man's eyes widened. "We were told the FBI shot him."

"Does it matter who shot him? He was a traitor. He deserved to die." He reached out. "Give me the gun."

"It does matter, Rahmed." The man stepped back. "How did Josef die?"

Raymond leaned with an outstretched hand as his foot eased away from her chest.

She could breathe again.

"Tell me what happened, Rahmed. Who killed Josef?"

Fury rose in Raymond's voice.

Maria shuddered. She knew that fury only too well.

"We are wasting time. I have to get to Layla.

That's all that matters. Give me the gun."

Daoud stepped farther away from Raymond. "It does matter. Tell me."

Raymond's voice was loud and commanding. "He betrayed the movement. That's what matters." Raymond's foot moved off her as he moved towards Daoud.

Maria stood up, her movements slow and sure. Her gaze never left Raymond.

His back was to her. In his anger over the other man's disrespect, he'd forgotten about her.

The cars. Surely, they hadn't had time to take the keys out. *Pick a car and go.*

She had to make her move. She ran.

"She's getting away," the man screamed as she slipped into the car.

She slammed the door shut and hit the lock button. Her hand moved to the ignition. Keys.

Thank you, God.

Raymond advanced with a gun in his hand.

The ignition sprang to life.

He raised the gun.

Her foot pressed against the gas pedal and the car surged forward.

Raymond jumped out of the way.

Seconds later, bullets slammed into the car.

52

One of the bullets must have hit the gas tank. The gasoline smell was strong

Maria kept driving, even knowing that.

On TV when bullets hit the gas tank, the car exploded into a gigantic fireball. Did such things happen in real life? It didn't matter.

Maria had no choice but to go on. Finding Layla was the only thing that mattered. If she stopped...she wouldn't think about that. Her foot pressed harder on the gas.

Raymond wouldn't catch up and get to Layla before she did.

She wouldn't allow that to happen. If she could get a few more miles before the car ran out of gas, she'd get out and hide. Her mind was numb, but she had to stay focused. *Layla is somewhere right this second and needs you.* But where was her little girl?

Her gaze shifted to the rearview mirror. A car was behind her in the distance—Raymond.

She rounded a sharp curve. The car's engine sputtered, and then died. All the gas had leaked out.

She only had seconds before Raymond's car would catch up. He would be sure to kill her this time. She opened the car door and ran across the open field.

As she heard the other car approaching, she fell to the ground. Her only hope was that he wouldn't waste time looking for her.

He wanted to get to Layla just as much as she did.

Without moving, she watched and prayed

Raymond's car stopped and both men got out. Raymond still had the gun in his hand.

His head turned and he seemed to be searching the field.

Please, God, don't let him see me. Please. Please. Her heart was in her throat. It seemed as if he stared directly at her. She fought the urge to jump up and run.

Finally, he turned back to the car. A moment later, the car drove away.

Maria jumped up and ran across the field to the road. Layla could be in any of the houses they'd passed, but she'd told her to go to a store or business.

She jogged down the road to a grove of pine trees. Going off road, she used the trees as cover. The scent of pine replaced the gagging smell of gasoline.

A building peeked through the trees. A tiny gas station. One of the old-fashioned kinds with one pump, a mechanic's bay, and nothing else. No fancy convenience store.

Every instinct screamed. *Layla was in that building.*

Raymond was already there. His car was parked in front. He was pounding on the door screaming.

Not wanting to alert Raymond, she slowed. Why would it be closed in the middle of the day?

Unless Layla had made it there and was hiding inside.

If she showed herself, he would shoot her, and then she wouldn't be able to help Layla. But watching him take her daughter again wasn't an option, either.

53

The squeal of sirens. The police would be here any moment.

Maria whispered, "Thank you, God." She would stay put as long as she could see Raymond. If he went inside the building, so would she.

Raymond turned towards the road. He'd obviously heard the sirens, as well. He yelled something to his companion.

Daoud went to Raymond and pulled on his arm as if urging him to leave.

Raymond shoved him away. A tug of war followed, but Raymond held his ground.

Daoud threw up his hands, and then jumped in the car and sped off the lot.

Raymond kicked at the glass door.

Hurry. Hurry. Where were they?

Maria moved closer to the station, but stayed hidden in the trees. There was no way she would stand here and watch Raymond take Layla. He might be stronger, but she would die to keep her daughter away from him.

Raymond's foot went through the glass. He reached into the hole. He would have Layla in a matter of seconds.

Police cars sped past.

Thank you, God. Help was finally here.

Layla would be safe.

Maria took off running.

Conrad jumped out of the car, running towards the station.

Zink leapt out from the other side, and a huge man stepped out from the back.

Maria blinked. Marcus Hanks. Here in Sunberry.

Nobody could hear her over the squealing of the sirens. She jogged towards them, grateful not to be alone.

Conrad pulled out his gun.

"Don't shoot." With the last of her strength, she dashed the rest of the way. "There's gasoline. You can't shoot. Don't."

Conrad turned towards her, but Suzanne lifted her gun.

Marcus moved forward as Suzanne covered him.

Maria kept running, screaming her daughter's name. Nobody would stop her from getting in there to get to Layla. She couldn't let Raymond have her.

Conrad's arms went around her. "You can't go in there."

She struggled against him. "Let me go. I have to. Layla might be in that building."

He held her firmly. "No."

She pushed on his chest, but couldn't break the bear hug. She crumpled in his arms, letting her tears flow. "Layla. Layla."

A gun shot from inside.

Raymond was shooting at them—at the police.

Maria's mind and heart froze. Her daughter might be in there.

More shots.

Maria stared.

Zink, Marcus, Ben Martin. All of them had their

guns aimed and firing. At Raymond in the station where Layla might be.

Couldn't breathe. She'd been so close, but Raymond had defeated her, sliced her heart from her chest. The pain sapped the strength from her knees. Her legs collapsed.

Conrad held her tight. "She wasn't in that building. I promise. Trust me." Conrad held her as she crumpled. "Look at me, Maria. Layla's fine."

"Oh, my precious little girl. Layla." The only thing keeping her standing was Conrad's arms around her. "He's got her. Raymond's got her."

"Maria, listen to me." Her gaze found his. "She's not in there."

"How do you know that?" His words penetrated her panic. Conrad wouldn't lie to her. She looked at him, hope rising.

"She called me. Just like you told her to." He held up his phone. "I asked her protector to take her somewhere safe while we dealt with the situation here."

Marcus moved closer to the station.

Ben and Suzanne stepped in sync behind him. All three had guns aimed.

Tears streamed down her face. "What if she didn't make it?"

He hugged her close. "She did. I need to go over there. Can I trust you to stay here and not put yourself or Layla in any more danger?"

An internal war waged inside her spirit.

Maria closed her eyes. *God, give me wisdom*

All of her wanted to run to her daughter's rescue. And all of her wanted to trust Conrad, but at one time she'd trusted Raymond. She'd vowed never to trust again, but Suzanne was right. Living without trust was like living in a dark world without beauty. You might survive, but that wasn't the same as living.

Beauty for ashes. God's promise.

She opened her eyes and met Conrad's gaze. "I trust you."

Conrad touched her cheek. "I will do everything in my power to keep her safe."

A chill hovered over her in spite of the warm day when Conrad moved towards the station. His gun was pulled and he moved up by Suzanne. Sudden silence.

Marcus's gun stayed leveled at the station's door. "It's over, Hamed. Throw out your gun."

Maria moved closer but stayed behind the cruisers.

"Where is my daughter? You have no right to keep her from me."

"You can see her after we get you in custody."

Over her dead body. Layla believed her dad was dead and she was going to keep on believing that. Maria took a step to move forward, but her gaze landed on Conrad. She stopped herself. No reason to charge in there. Conrad would take care of the situation.

"I don't believe you." Raymond called out from the station.

"Well, you can believe this, Hamed." Marcus's voice rang out, loudly and clearly. The righteous anger in his voice told Maria he hadn't known Raymond was alive any more than she had. "You won't see her until you put down that gun and come out with your hands up."

It was quiet for a moment, and then Raymond gave his answer. He shot at Marcus, but Marcus hit the ground and the bullet missed.

In the next second, a hail of gunfire split the air.

It seemed as if it went on forever, but then the guns fell silent.

Marcus called out.

No response.

54

Maria walked into the old gas station.

Her gaze moved to Raymond's body. Her stomach twisted at the pools of blood.

Conrad moved to her and put a hand on her arm. "It's over. Really over. He won't hurt you or Layla ever again."

She nodded. "Or anyone else."

Suzanne walked up to her. "Do you want to feel for a pulse this time?"

Maria looked down. "That won't be necessary."

Conrad put an arm around her and led her out of the station. "Look over there."

Her daughter barreled across the yard from the small house beside the station. A strange man jogged behind her.

Layla's arms were up in the air. "Mommy. Mommy."

Maria fell to her knees and scooped Layla into her embrace. Her daughter's arms went round her neck as Layla nuzzled closer. Tears flowed from Maria. "Oh, thank you, God for keeping my Layla safe."

"And thank you for keeping my mommy safe, too, God. I love her so much." Layla's arms squeezed around her neck. Maria thought she may never let her go again—ever.

Conrad put a hand on Maria's shoulder.

She looked up into his warm smiling eyes. "And

thank you."

"I didn't do anything. You and Layla did all the hard work."

"You promised you'd bring Layla home and you did."

"I always keep my promises. Or at least I do my best. I can't say it always works out this well." Conrad winked. "This is a really, exceptional day."

"I don't understand. I...thought you were in there." She hugged Layla close.

"We were, but we heard the bad man kicking on the door so Mr. Grappler took me to his house to keep me safe."

She didn't want to know the answer but she had to ask the question. "Did you see the bad man?" If her daughter had to mourn the death of her father again, it would be a tragedy. Maria changed her thought—sad but not a tragedy. With God's help, Raymond's hatred would never touch Layla's sweet heart again.

Mr. Grappler shook his head. "No. We heard a lot of screaming, but we couldn't see what was happening. We sneaked out the back and went to the house just before the bad guy got in."

Maria stood up. "Oh, no. Your gas station is practically destroyed."

"Doesn't matter. I've been looking for an excuse to move to warmer weather, anyway. And now I can say I'm a bona fide hero."

"Yes, you can." Maria hugged him. "In fact I seem to be surrounded by heroes."

Marcus Hanks walked up.

She glared at him. "We need to talk."

"And we will, but not in front of Layla. But I do want to tell you that I didn't lie. I had no idea."

Did she believe him?

The answer to her question came unbidden. There were good people who wanted to help her. If only she would let them.

She smiled at Marcus. "I believe you."

He smiled back.

No one was meant to be alone. It was time to trust the people God put in her life. Her hand moved to Conrad's.

His strong, warm fingers encircled hers.

55

"Wake up, sleepy head." Maria sat on the bed she shared with Layla at Suzanne's. It would be awhile before she let her daughter out of her sight—if ever. "I have a surprise for you."

"What's the surprise?" Layla rubbed her eyes.

"If I tell you, it won't be a surprise. Now get up and get moving." She smiled at the recollection of Suzanne using those same exact words a few days earlier. "And besides, I don't know what the surprise is, either. Miss Suzanne told me to get showered and get ready for a surprise. A really, big surprise."

Layla jumped off the bed. "Let's hurry, Mommy. I love surprises."

Maria was glad to see Layla had no apparent trauma from her ordeal.

According to Marcus, heads were rolling in very high places. Even though it was widely spread that Raymond had died from the gunshot wound, it had been a lie—a hoax. An elaborate sting operation was planned with Raymond helping catch terrorists from a country that was considered more of a threat than his. Somehow, Raymond faked his death during the operation.

David Hamed called his brother's friends to take vengeance for Raymond and Josef's death. That set the wheels in motion for Raymond to come back and take his daughter. His fellow terrorists contacted Raymond.

Thankfully, it had taken more time to set up the operation than they'd believed or Layla wouldn't have still been at that broken down motel that day.

Raymond died this time, a shot straight to the heart from Suzanne's gun as he'd struggled with Marcus and Suzanne inside the gas station's mechanic's bay.

With that knowledge came peace. Raymond, so filled with hate and evil intent towards his enemies, would never see his daughter grow up.

Maria towel-dried Layla's hair and waited for her to dress.

Maria's jaw dropped as she entered the room, to see Jamie Jakowski and her twin, Patti. Jamie's daughter was Layla's cousin since their fathers had been brothers. Maria hadn't been allowed to contact them after she and Layla disappeared.

Jamie and Patti jumped off the couch and yelled in unison. "Surprise!"

Layla ran to her aunts, if not in blood in spirit.

The three women had made the choice to be sisters in spite of the pain that bound them together.

Maria smiled—there was that beauty for ashes thing again. A definite theme in her life.

"Where's Sabrina?" Layla shouted, not waiting for them to answer as she started telling them about the bad man.

Patti and Jamie asked questions and told her what a brave little girl she was.

"My name is Jasmine now. But I like to be called Jazzy."

Patti hugged her. "No need, Layla. Everyone knows that's your name."

She turned towards her mother. "But I love the name Jazzy."

Maria laughed. "Fine, then you can keep it. Use it as your nickname. How's that?"

Layla put her hand on her hip and gave her mother a look.

"How's that, Jazzy?"

"Thank you, Mommy. Where's Sabrina?"

"She's in the barn with Miss Suzanne."

"Can I go?"

Maria nodded and watched as she ran out the sliding glass door. "Oh my goodness." Maria exclaimed. "That is quite the surprise. How did you even know where I was?"

"We saw the whole thing play out on TV," Patti said as she hugged Maria again. "We would have been here sooner, but a certain FBI agent said it would be better if we waited."

"Marcus?"

"Yeah, and then he came up here without us." Jamie gritted her teeth. As a former FBI agent, it was obvious she didn't like being out of the loop.

"That was probably a good thing knowing how much trouble the two of you can get into. I can't believe you're here."

She looked at the twin sisters who looked nothing like each other. Jamie's hair had been chopped short and dyed red. Patti's brown hair was long and curly with blonde highlights.

"That's quite the do, Jamie."

Jamie fluffed at ginger-colored bangs. "Like it?"

"It's an interesting look."

"Even though I'm a stay-at-home mom right now, I decided to do something wild with my hair.

According to Patti, I'm simply in denial about my age and the fact that I'm getting old."

"That is not what I said."

Jamie shrugged. "Really? Cause that's what I heard."

Conrad called from the kitchen. "Breakfast will be ready in a minute."

Maria extricated herself from Patti's hug and walked to the kitchen.

She wouldn't have survived Layla's kidnapping without Conrad and Suzanne. One or the other had been with her every moment. "Hey, I didn't know you were here."

"Where else would I be?" He smiled and touched her cheek. "Not only here, but assigned to cooking detail."

"Good, I'm starving." Jamie called from the living room.

"Nothing new about that, sis. You are always starving. I wish I could eat the way she does." Patti laughed.

"You could. We have the same genes, remember?"

"So you say, but I'm pretty sure if I ate the way you do, I'd weigh five hundred pounds."

"So, what? Now that you're happily married what difference does it make?" Jamie laughed. "Carter's so in love with you that he won't care."

Maria poked her head out of the kitchen. "You're married?"

Patti nodded. "We are. It was a beautiful wedding. We would have invited you...but well...you know. We didn't know where you were. It's been three months now." Patti held up her hand. An antique diamond solitaire rested on her finger.

"That's wonderful. I'm so happy for the two of you."

"Not as happy as they are." Jamie winked. "The two of them are so happy it's almost sickening."

"You're just jealous."

"Am not."

The back door opened. Sabrina and Layla ran in ahead of Suzanne. Layla skidded to a stop, grabbed her cousin's hand, and looked up at Maria. "This is a good surprise, isn't it, Mommy?"

"The best."

Conrad walked in with plates. "OK, I've got sausage and bacon. Now eat before all my hard work gets cold."

****

After breakfast, the girls ran outside to play with the promise of the back yard only. No woods.

Maria still needed to see Layla at any given moment.

The adults sat around the table listening to how Patti and Jamie met Maria.

Jamie grabbed Maria's hand. "I am so sorry for all that you've gone through. I can't believe the FBI lied to—"

"I know, Jamie. It was tough, but it ended well. And it's not your fault. I'm done dwelling on the past."

Jamie nodded. "I know, but..."

"Face it. We made stupid choices for the fathers of our children. It's something we will always have to live with. But I'm done letting it define me or Layla."

"Wow. That is a great attitude, Maria." Patti placed her coffee cup on the table.

"It is, isn't it? It's all about God and trust. If you believe God loves you and you believe God is good, the trusting Him in the bad times comes a lot easier."

"How'd you get so wise?"

Maria pointed back towards the kitchen where Conrad and Suzanne were. "God put some amazing people in my life right when I needed them the most. I couldn't have survived without them."

"I'm glad about that and I have no plan of letting you disappear from our lives again." Jamie told her. "Family sticks together, right?"

"That's right. We are sisters by choice." Patti smiled as Conrad and Suzanne walked back into the room.

Suzanne gathered up dirty dishes. "I still can't believe Raymond's brother refused to give up."

"At least the policeman he shot will live. Unlike him." Conrad's voice held no sympathy. "I guess he didn't want to go to an American prison for killing the newscaster."

Patti shook her head. "The whole thing is crazy. I can't believe it. A few weeks ago he was just another college kid here on a visa, and then he turns into a homicidal maniac with only one goal."

"To kidnap Layla," Maria said.

Suzanne walked out to the kitchen, but stopped at the doorway and turned back to them. "Talk about family loyalty."

Conrad put his hand over Maria's and smiled at her. "Yeah, family loyalty is all well and good, but that's a little extreme."

Maria stood up. "I'm sorry, Suzanne. How inconsiderate of us to be talking about all this."

"Don't be silly. I'm thrilled that Emily and Layla

are back at home with their parents where they belong. One day it will be my turn."

"I know, but it still has to be tough."

"Why is that?" Jamie looked from Maria to Suzanne.

Suzanne turned towards her. Her violet blue eyes were shiny, but her voice was in control as she explained, "My husband kidnapped my son two years ago. We haven't been able to find either of them yet."

Jamie half-stood, but then sat back down. "Really. I want to hear the details—if you don't mind. "

Patti shook her head. "No, Jamie. You're retired, remember?"

Jamie smiled. "I know that. But if I can help, what would be wrong with that?"

"Nothing, if you don't put yourself in danger."

After Jamie hugged her sister, she grabbed some plates to help clear the table. "I have no plans to do that." She looked at Suzanne. "We'll talk later."

Patti and Maria looked at each other, and then at Jamie. At the same time, they said, "You're retired."

"Someone probably needs to tell her that." Conrad told the women with a smile.

Patti sighed. "I do—all the time."

****

Maria stood at the window watching Layla and Sabrina playing outside Suzanne's house. The others sat around the table laughing and talking while having a second up of coffee.

Conrad walked over and placed his arm around her shoulder. "She's safe now."

She smiled up at him. "Call me a helicopter mom

if you will, but I like my eyes on her."

"Can't say that I blame you. So...what are you going to do now?"

"Witness Protection wants me to stay in the program. Even with Raymond dead, they can't be sure there aren't others out there like his brother."

He nodded. "Makes sense." His voice was noncommittal.

"But I really like Sunberry and the people who live here."

"Anyone in particular?" He gently picked up her hand

"Several come to mind. Emily and her parents. Suzanne. Ben Martin. Even my nosy neighbor."

"That's it. What about me?"

"I..." She looked away, suddenly feeling shy and unsure.

Conrad clasped her hand tighter. "Let me make this easy on you. I like you and I want nothing more than to get to know you and Layla, but staying here will put you at risk. I can't ask that. I understand that your job is to keep Layla safe. "

Maria turned towards him. "You're not asking. I'm not running anymore. If I've learned anything over the past few weeks, I know I can't hide. If someone wants to find me, they will. This is a good town with good people. And I like it here."

"You're not going into Witness Protection?"

"I told them yesterday."

His arms went around her. "That is the best news I've heard in a long time. I might just get to ask you to one of the Bucks' games after all."

She stepped closer, not sure what the future held. But it would be good whatever it was. God had

promised beauty for her ashes.
    "And I might just say yes."

Thank you for purchasing this Harbourlight title. For other inspirational stories, please visit our on-line bookstore at www.pelicanbookgroup.com.

For questions or more information, contact us at customer@pelicanbookgroup.com.

Harbourlight Books
The Beacon in Christian Fiction™
an imprint of Pelican Ventures Book Group
www.pelicanbookgroup.com

May God's glory shine through
this inspirational work of fiction.

AMDG